CHILD
—of—
Dawn

LESLIE A LEE

Copyright © 2023 Leslie A Lee.
All rights reserved.

Dedication

To those who believe in the beauty within the things we can see and things which we cannot.
For my children.
For my parents.
For the warrior women in my life.
And
For Hunter—who reminded me that weird is good, and imagination is everything.

AUTHOR'S NOTE:

I hope that my readers come with imagination
and a desire to leave this world for a bit.
In case you are unaware, dear reader, those living in other
worlds have fantastical names. And as such, the reader may
wonder what those names mean. Because of this, I have
enclosed the meanings of the names of people, places, and
things to help you further enjoy this tale. All names are
either Norwegian, Scandinavian, Germanic, or Gaelic.
However, one might also find a bit of elvish thrown in.
Enjoy the journey.
Never stop believing.

Name	Who, What, Where	Meaning
(In alphabetical order)		
Anda	Half elf, half human	Bold Journey
Asestein	A seeing stone	Seeing Stone
Bearla	Elvish princess	Glow
Calina	Elvish kingdom	Fog
Ciallhmar	Elvish Seer	Wise
Cleite	The sacred vampire tree	Feather
Dagsbrún	Half vampire, half elf	First Light of Day
Dhia	Magical elvish being	God
Dorchadas	Vampire kingdom	Darkness
Droime	A Kelpie	Running
Drotinn	An elf	Leader
Erik	Stolthet's husband	Ruler
Forbindelse	A magical connection Between two beings	Connection
Gammel	An ancient elf	Old
Gréasáin	The ancient web that connects all things.	Web
Gudinne	One of the Vondod	Goddess
Ljosalfar	An elf, Dagsbrún's mother	Light elf
Lys	An elf, Anda's mother	Light
Morsdog	One of the Vondod	Mother
Naofa	Sacred elvish forest	Sacred
Raefn	A vampire, Dagsbrún's father	Source of light
Realtai	Wampyr's mate	Star
Regelen	Ancient elvish book of laws	Arrange

Rioghail	Elvish prince	Regal
Scath	Vampire Castle	Shadow
Skaperen	Elf who wrote the *Regelen*	Maker
Skog	Dagsbrún's castle	Forest
Stolthet	Anda's sister	The pride of something fine
Suiochan Ard	Elvish Castle	High Seat
Sybil	One of the Vondod	Oracle
Tvil	Village where Anda grew up	Uncertain
Uvl	Anda's father	Wolf
Vandre	Gypsy human, Dagsbrún's servant	To walk far.
Vind Tunge	Magical language	The wind tongue
Vondod	The Undead	Pain
Wampyr	Leader of the vampires	Old English for vampire

Prologue

People would speak of that night as one filled rampant with magic. The realms of the spirits lowered their veils and revealed all manner of mystery in the dark shadows of twilight. In the darkness, the dogs howled at the bright, gilded orb of the moon and serenaded the spirits that left their homes to walk among mortals. Perhaps it was the moon that drew them out, perhaps it was their restless nature to wander… or perhaps they fled the tumult that raged behind the shroud draped over those lands we cannot see.

Draped in secrecy, the immortal world was boiling and surging with whispers. Whispers that the unthinkable had happened. A creature of light had given themselves to a creature of the night. What else could have caused the storms, the raging thunder? What else could account for trees to leave their roots or the rivers to rise and clash with the mountains? It was unthinkable, forbidden, blasphemy, but it was the only explanation. And so, lips moved, and tongues wagged from pointed ears to curved horns like the lightning that flashed across the sky. It coursed through the very fabric of the landscape, threatening to rip apart the very fiber of the immortal world.

The Elders chased the whispers through the night to a cave buried deep in the dark forest. They felt the ground beneath them writhe with confusion and fear as they dug their gnarled and aged staffs into the soft earth. They came from the Shadowlands and the Lakelands; they came in shimmery robes and blackened capes. The thought that two of their own had defied their ancient rules had united them and thrust them together in a frenzied state.

They crashed like beasts through the tangled wood until they came upon the cave. The air was alive with electricity, stretched and strained with uncertainty. They stopped, ceasing their commotion so that the only sound was the sigh of the wind as it consoled the leaves in the weeping trees. One elder moved into a sliver of moonlight that fell over the mouth of the cave. He was old and wizened, well past his days of glory and well into his time of twilight. Others moved to join him, but he raised his hand, and they stopped.

The elder slipped his head under the rocky archway and into the inky darkness of the cave. Shadows mixed with moonlight and played tricks on his weary eyes. He strained his ears to hear even the faintest sound, secretly hoping that he would not. But his hopes were in vain, and he shut his eyes in despair as a muffled cry echoed against the stony walls. He threw his staff hard against the ground, and its tip erupted into a flaming torch. Shadows leaped back into the crevices as light flowed up to the topmost part of the cave. The only shadow that remained unfolded itself against the luminous rays of light and stretched its limbs out in search of a place to hide. The elder followed its path up into the rocky crags and then lowered his eyes back to the ground.

"It's no use," he called to the shadow. "We know your secret."

The shadow seemed to dip back into the earth, only to spring up once more in the shape of a man. An immense figure of stony white skin, rough and hewn like the rocks he walked among. His chiseled form was draped in a robe of deep purple, and the folds rolled over the ground and melted into its shape. He pulled himself up to his full height and stared at the elder with steely blue eyes.

"You have no business here, old man," he hissed.

"You made it my business!" the elder yelled back. "You broke every law this world has ever known."

Before the elder could blink, he found himself pinned against the cold, hard wall of the cave. An iron grip was pressing the life from his throat. He looked down into the blazing eyes of his opponent, grasping at the gnarled hands that trapped him. The shadow that had melded into a man now looked more like a beast in the torchlight. His ears were curved to a delicate point, and his front teeth sharpened to crystal tips. The elder heard scratching on either side of him and turned to see a claw, glistening black like the granite stone, scraping along the surface of the stone towards his face. The elder could see that the claw was connected to the tip of a wing, a wing that had billowed forth from the creature's back. Turning his head, he could see that the wing had a match, and those wings now enveloped him in their dark, inky beauty.

"Your magic has no power here, old man," the creature snarled. "We do not listen to your legalistic preaching."

The elder felt himself drifting off into the darkness. His hands fell away from the creature's grip on his throat. "Where is she?" he gasped. "Where is Ljosalfar?"

Before the creature could respond, a voice answered for him. "I am here."

Both the elder and the creature turned and watched as the figure of a woman moved from behind a tall boulder. She seemed to float across the earth as she drifted toward them. She reached out and touched the arm of the creature. Without argument, the creature released his grip on the elder and let him drop to the ground.

The elder gasped for breath and pushed himself up with the help of his staff. "You are marked," he whispered hoarsely. "Even now, elders from both your worlds are gathered outside. There is no escape."

The creature reached out with a wing and enveloped the woman, pulling her close. "We will not leave. We are bonded. We have hand fasted."

The elder's face grew pale. "And who oversaw this union? Who else has played a part in this witchcraft?

"No one," the woman replied. "No one would have us."

Voices could be heard outside and the elder knew he was losing time. He reached out to the woman. "Ljosalfar, please." She pulled away from his reach. "You are Faye, you are my blood. Do not remain with this beast." His eyes filled with tears. "It will be your destruction."

The creature pulled his wing tighter around Ljosalfar. "Then she will die in my arms."

The elder saw uncertainty creep into the green pools of her eyes. "Granddaughter, I beg you. If the elders enter this cave, I will be unable to protect you, or him."

Ljosalfar's eyes misted and brimmed with tears. She looked up at her mate and then back at the elder. Slowly she pulled the folds of her cloak away from her body and lifted a small bundle off her shoulder. She handed it to the elder. "And what of the child? What will become of him?"

The elder felt his heart leap and then plummet as he took the small bundle. He lifted the gauzy wrap away from a face that was formed into perfection. The child was a mere infant, no more than a few days old. Its eyelashes, dark like a raven's wing, were draped over sleeping eyes. Though a newborn, the child had thick, curly locks that cascaded in loose curls over pointy ears. Its skin was a grayish white, like a slab of marble newly cut from the earth.

He felt his soul shattered as he clutched the infant. "Ljosalfar," he whispered. "What have you done?"

"He is ours," the creature replied. "A union of two worlds. Proof that love exists beyond the confines you have given it."

"Take him," Ljosalfar pushed the infant against the elder's chest. "Hide him, please."

Voices echoed at the entrance to the cave, and the creature pulled Ljosalfar against him. "Do as she says, old man. For the sake of your granddaughter and great-grandchild, do this one thing you know to be right." He lowered one wing and pushed the elder with his other toward the back of the cave. "There is a small opening. Take the child, hide him, and give him the possibility of a life we were never offered."

The cave grew brighter with the light of the approaching torches. Ljosalfar pushed the elder toward the back of the cave. "Go!" she screamed. "Go!"

The elder stumbled back as the creature grabbed Ljosalfar and enveloped her in his wings. They turned toward the mob, now filling the room with their torches. The elder ducked behind a stone. He held the child close and peered around the corner of his hiding place.

"Where is Drotinn?" an elf yelled, flailing his torch in the face of the creature.

A darkly robbed figure approached from the rear, and the throng parted. He removed his hood, and the elder saw that he looked much like the father of the child he now held in his arms. Standing only a few inches from the creature. He gripped one of his wings in his hands and snapped it in half. The creature howled in pain but held Ljosalfar even more tightly with his other wing.

"The elf asked you a question," the figure hissed. "Where is the elder?"

"Gone," the creature growled. "Gone. And with our child."

The figure let out an unearthly scream. "Traitor! Blasphemer! You have broken all our laws! You have upset the balance of our world!" He drew a long, metal stake from the folds of his cloak. "And for that, you and your harlot will pay." Without uttering another breath, he took the stake and drove through Ljosalfar into the heart of the creature.

The elder covered his mouth to muffle his cries of anguish. He turned and felt his way through the darkness until his hand felt the night air pull him out into the anguished night. Stumbling blindly, he uttered an incantation to shut the cave walls and give him a chance to escape. His life was forever changed. He would be a hunted thing, sought after like a hunted animal. But, as he fled into the night, he knew that his life was bearable compared to the agony of the child's parents.

Inside the cave, the mob had grown silent, almost out of some inexplicable reverence for the fate of the two lovers. The creature had fallen back to the earth, lit from the inside with a fire that was slowly burning him to death. He held Ljosalfar in his arms, and she too began to glimmer with a hot white light.

"It burns," she cried out, clawing at the creature's arms.

He grabbed her hand and held it against his burning chest. "Shh, my love. It will be over soon."

Ljosalfar writhed against her agony. "I love you, Raefn," she whispered. Her body grew bright and erupted in a fountain of light and heat. Its flame leaped upward and then faded into an ethereal glow. Remnants of light drifted down and fell upon the creature's face, dissipating into steam as they fell upon his tears.

The creature threw his head back and roared. He reached up, grasping at the pieces of light falling back down to the earth. His body grew brighter from the flame burning him alive. He looked at the mob, many of whom now second-guessed their decision, and then raised his good wing to its full height and slammed it down to the earth. Its power threw the mob backward, knocking them to the ground. He grasped the last remnant of light, held it to his heart, and erupted into an inferno of flame and ash.

Chapter 1

The vapors came on the winds of wagging tongues and breezes of rumor. Creeping out of the crags of the mountains and bowels of the earth, it came quietly into the village, blanketing it in unrest and uneasiness. It settled on the thatched rooftops and curled itself about the chimneys, mingling with the early morning smoke as it rose from dying embers. It swirled about the hooves of the livestock, causing them to shift from one foot to another in a constant dance of uncertainty.

The people of Tvil needed little help in finding anything to be suspicious of, as they were known for their skepticism and doubt. Living in the shadow of the Black Mountains, they were prone to always believe some evil was upon them, even though the Vale had not been broken in many years. And yet, they still clacked like worried hens about what the next malady might be that would befall them. They shuffled in and out of the shadows and whispered behind closed doors, always looking for someone to blame, always conspiring who they would punish.

And all eyes would turn to the north of the village, to the very edge where a farm sat apart from the rest of the buildings. Here, the earth grasses met the trees, and the sheep would cease to graze. Here, the forests began, and somewhere, lost in its wooden folds, lay the Vale – the invisible entrance to the supernatural otherworld of beings spoken of in stories. Man did not cross over there, nor did those beings cross over into the world of men… save when the Vale saw fit to permit it. The villagers saw this as a dark and wicked magic, bringing only things of evil into their world.

Ulv did not agree with this notion.

As the owner of the farm in question, he had never seen anything of such evil come through the Vale. Indeed, the only thing he had seen traverse the Vale was anything but evil. Indeed, she was all that was good and perfect in his mind. Ulv would never forget the day that Lys had stumbled from the otherworld into his own. It had been a wild and ravenous night where the wind clawed at the tall grasses as it swooped down from the Black Mountains. Ulv had been trying in vain to find one of his lambs that had strayed from the herd in fright. As he had struggled through the wall of rain, he had heard the little lamb bleating and had followed its cries. Through what seemed to be a part in the downpour, he saw the lamb cradled in a woman's arms. The water poured down around her but did not land on her porcelain skin. Her hair cascaded in wild waves over her shoulders and covered the lamb in a golden blanket.

Ulv was entranced by her presence, knowing at once this must be a creature from the Vale. She looked at him, and he was surprised to see fear in her eyes. He had always believed these creatures to be superior to emotion. A gust of wind swelled up behind her and caused her to stumble. She staggered toward him, clutching the bleating lamb to her chest. He reached out to catch her, and she fell into her arms. Her limbs were lifeless, but there was still warmth in her body. He caught her up and carried her back to his farm.

Lys had no memory of her journey through the Vale. One moment, she had been in her world; the next she was in the storm, holding the lamb. She was a creature of few words, but Ulv did not mind. Her gentle spirit and tender heart made her company pleasant. She filled his dreary home with an airy light and put a joy in his heart he had never known. She made him laugh, a deep, rolling laugh that echoed alongside hers. Ulv found himself fearful of Lys' return through the Vale, unable to imagine what life could possibly be like without her there.

To his joy, Lys seemed to have no desire to return home. From the few words she shared with him, she had been some sort of outcast, though Ulv could not imagine why. She seemed to be the embodiment of all that could be good and wonderful. And so, Ulv asked her to be his wife. To his joy and relief, Lys agreed. They were married by a priest in a tiny hollow with no guests in attendance. The villagers were wary of Lys, believing her to be a poor omen. They blamed her arrival on all manner of maladies – from crops wilting to leaky roofs. Ulv was enraged by their childish behavior, but Lys seemed blissfully unaware that her presence was unwelcome in the village.

A year later, they welcomed their first daughter, Stolthet. She was born on an airy spring day, full of fragrance and sunlight. She never cried, never was irritable or out of sorts. Indeed, the villager whispered that she surely must be enchanted with magic from her mother's world, so flawless and perfect she was. Three years later, Lys told Ulv and Stolthet that they would once more welcome a little one into their family. Stolthet and her father were beside themselves with joy.

But the joy was not meant to last.

For while Lys' delivery of Stolthet was filled with nothing but ease, her second one was fraught with pain. The baby came in the middle of winter, and only the snowdrift and howl of hungry wolves welcomed it. Lys writhed and moaned in distress, for no physician would come to aid her. Ulv watched, helpless, unable to help the woman he had come so desperately to love. Stolthet huddled in the corner, terrified of her mother's moans and howl of the wolves as they circled outside. When the baby came, Ulv cradled Lys' head with one hand and caught his newborn daughter with the other. The baby issued a muffled cry, and Lys sighed.

"Anda, her name is Anda," she whispered. "I give her my last breath, so that she may breathe her first." It was the most she had ever said to Ulv. And the last thing he ever heard passed from her lips.

Ulv felt his soul immeasurably wither. Lys' light dimmed, leaving her skin ashen like willow bark. He lay his beloved's head gently on their bed and stood to cradle his daughter in his arms. Crossing the room, he reached into the cradle he had lovingly made for her and pulled out a small carving of a wolf. Placing it against her cheek, he sank into a chair and wept.

Stolthet whimpered and crawled up on his lap. Outside, the winds quieted, and the wolves howling turned to a soft cry. Ulv looked at his two daughters through his tears, his heart overwhelmed with agony. "Do you hear?" he cried. "All of nature knows our sorrow." He hugged them both tightly. "Yes, Anda, daughter of the wolf and the light...all of nature knows the darkness you were born into."

It was not simple to raise two daughters as a farmer, but Ulv did the best he could. The girls learned at a young age that the village saw both them and their mother as different. While they would never say so to their faces, they would whisper behind Stolthet and Anda's backs. One was enchanted with her perfect looks and graces, while the other was cursed because her birth had killed her mother. They were the subject of taunting at school, and mockery in the village square. Ulv would challenge anyone whom he heard slander his children, and so it was always done in whispers. As they grew older, the sisters learned to ignore the wagging tongues for they knew in their hearts that the villagers were fools and their mother had been nothing more than someone who loved them completely.

The seasons turned and Stolthet proved that despite her reputation she was a desirable young lady. The young men of the village found her intelligence and wit intriguing and soon many were vying for her hand in marriage. While Ulv raised an eyebrow at each of them, he could not argue that it would be welcoming to have a son to aid in the work around the farm. Winter was growing colder in his bones, and he saw an aging man in his reflection in the water.

So, when Stolthet accepted the hand of Erik, Ulv was almost relieved. Erik genuinely seemed to care for his eldest daughter and was willing to take on the burden of running the farm alongside Ulv. Stolthet beamed with happiness and fully became the woman of the house, replacing her mother in all but memory. An atmosphere of happiness seemed to settle over the farm and little family. Everyone seemed content.

Everyone except Anda.

While her father and sister had tried to shield her from the truth, she had grown with the knowledge of knowing that her life cost her mother her own. And while she knew those who mattered had never blamed her, she was very aware of the curse people believed her to be. While her sister was fair-haired and skinned, she possessed hair that caught the flame of the sun and skin dappled in freckles. There was no reason for this, and therefore it was whispered that she possessed the magic her mother seemed to have lost when she crossed the Vale. Ulv openly scoffed at this notion, but secretly wondered if Lys had given some sort of secret enchantment to their youngest child.

Truly, she lived as though she were bewitched. She grew further out of what was normal, and deeper into a world of her own. She was whimsical and out of place with the other youth. Her temper raged against those who mocked her and Stolthet. She found her solace in the depths of the tall grasses and crevices of the Black Mountains. She was more a wild creature than she was a young woman. All of nature seemed synchronized with her soul. The wind moaned at her sadness and the birds sang at her joy.

And so, when the mists came, the village could only blame her. They crested over the Black Mountains and crept from the darkness of the woods. Their very source seemed to be those locales that were cursed and therefore surely these mists were a plague upon the village. The villagers in their virtue could think of nothing they had done to reap such a punishment, and so they surmised that Anda had caused this spell out of the evilness of her heart. They grumbled during the day and plotted against her and her family by firelight in the dark.

Ulv was immovable. He would not leave his home, nor uproot his daughter and new son-in-law. The farm was their inheritance, their birthright. He had nothing but the land to give them and the village would not deny him that right. And yet, as the mists lingered, his heart began to realize the agonizing truth that his youngest was no longer safe in his care. And so, one evening, as the sun settled in the cradle of the golden peaks, he went in search of her. He found her where he knew he would, in the barn, speaking quiet mutterings to the horses. Her hair and clothes were covered with bits of hay, and she smelt of fresh earth and grass.

"Anda."

She turned at the sound of her name on her father's tongue. "Da, come look. The mare has silver in her mane. See how It sparkles in the twilight?" Anda caressed the mare's forehead with so much tenderness, that Ulv questioned himself. "Even in the elder of her years, there is magic within her."

"Age brings an elegant refinement to those creatures who accept it with grace," Ulv stroked the mare's neck. "Anda, we must speak."

She turned away from the mare. "Yes, Da?"

Ulv tried to swallow the blocks in his throat. "Anda, it is no longer safe for you here." A cloud passed over her face, and Ulv noticed how the shadows grew longer on the ground. "Daughter, you must know the whispers spoken about you in the village. And I fear for you."

Anda's face was unreadable. She crossed the barn and stood in the doorway. "What would you have me do, Da?"

His throat tightened. "Your mother did not come from here…"

"This I know."

Her brusque reply only unnerved him more. "Indeed, your mother was not of this world. And perhaps that is why you feel yourself so at odds with life here." Ulv knew his words were not what his heart meant to say. "Perhaps you could find happiness elsewhere."

"Happiness?" The word seemed to choke her.

Ulv felt his entire body sag. "At least you would be safe. Your mother gave you a gift, but I do not know how you can use it here."

Anda lowered her eyes. "I do not know what this gift you speak of is. Indeed, I am more cursed than gifted."

He caught her up in a swift hug. "Do not ever say you are cursed. Your mother gave you something that was as much a part of her as if she had given you her own heart. But Anda, there are people who cannot see what is extraordinary, only what is ordinary. And therefore, they would destroy you simply because they cannot understand you."

A dim rumbling echoed against the foot of the Black Mountains and reverberated through the walls of the barn. Ulv turned to see what appeared to be fireflies crossing the fields between the village and his farm. The tiny lights rose and fell over the tall grasses like a luminescent wave. The rumble seemed to rise and fall with them. And then, Ulv felt an icy chill curl up and around his spine and shatter like ice in his heart. He grabbed Anda and pulled her back into the barn.

"Da!" Anda cried out in surprise.

"Anda," Ulv squeezed her shoulder. "You must run. Run!" He saw fear race across her face and fill her eyes. "Anda, they are coming. Now. At this very moment. They are coming now. For you."

"Da," tears welled in her eyes. "Da I do not want to go!"

He pulled her to the back of the barn and threw open a small door. "You must run into the woods."

Her eyes widened. "But they are forbidden!"

Ulv pulled a cloak from a peg and wrapped her in it. "To man, yes. But to you…" He fastened the cloak and pulled the hood up over his head. "To you, they will be a sanctuary. For you are not wholly of this world. And that will be your salvation."

Anda sank against her father and wept. "I do not want to leave you."

He tilted her chin up toward his own and gazed into her eye for what he believed would be the last time. "Your mother gave you breath with her last one. I will not be the one to see it removed from your body." He kissed her forehead and pushed her out into the night. He knew he would die with the image of her disconsolate face etched into his memory. He memorized each line and curve, each freckle and curl, wishing he had done so before this moment. And then, with a strength not his own, he slammed the door and shut his daughter out in the cloak of the shadows.

Chapter 2

Vandre was born in the crook of the earth's arms. His mother dug a small burrow, lined it with branches, and brought him into the world on her own. She cleaned his tiny body in the water of the stream, wrapped him in her skirt, and rushed to catch up with the caravan she traveled with. For Vandre was born into the world of gypsies—nomads of the world, and the ragamuffins of society. His father never made himself known, and so his mother was often pushed to the edges of her wandering tribe. Her beauty made her a target for both men and women – one out of jealousy, and the other out of lust. And while she tried her best to keep to herself, she often found herself, amid all manner of commotion and chaos.

Vandre grew to be a quiet and sullen youth, aware that his mother's circumstances made him a pariah. He learned to be silent and to keep his head lowered to where his eyes could not find trouble. He taught himself from the ragged books in the back of his mother's wagon, refusing to accept the ignorance of the gypsies as his fate. He read of the stars and how they moved with the dance of the earth. He read of the path the world traversed within the sky. And he read of the realms beyond the site of man and the magical wonder that existed there. Vandre would often wander away from the caravan and imagine he walked alongside the Vale, wishing he could inadvertently step from this world into another. He often believed that he could hear creatures conversing just beyond the invisible barrier and wished more than anything to be a part of their conversation. He often lost himself in imaginary conversations that were far grander than any he could have with any of his fellow gypsies.

It was during one of these imaginary dialogues that he found himself interrupted by the sound of cries from the woods. He opened his eyes to be greeted by plumes of smoke snaking into the sky. Its pungent smell bit at his nose as he leaped to his feet and plunged into the woods. The cries grew louder, and bits of orange flame could be seen through the wooded trees. He crashed into the clearing where the gypsy camp had been pitched to find them all in a state of chaos. Men were throwing helpless buckets of water on indomitable flames as the women tried to snuff them out with strips of cloth. He wove through the madness toward his mother's wagon.

In front of it, a small crowd of half a dozen gypsies stood watching two men grapple at one another with raging and clenched fists. The smaller of the two was bloodied from head to toe, but still standing, willing himself onward with strength past what he humanely contained. His adversary who was far less winded swung and hit and wrestled with an ease that made his attempts almost comical in appearance. Vandre inquired of one of the bystanders as to the whereabouts of his mother and they pointed around the back of their wagon.

Vandre rounded the corner of the wagon and felt his body freeze in horror. One of the older women cradled his mother's head in her lap. His mother's hand gripped a wound in her chest between her ribs. Blood trickled over fingers like liquid rubies as it caught the light of the flames. Vandre sank to his knees and placed his hands over her own.

"Mama?"

His mother groaned but did not respond.

He looked to the old woman for answers. She shook her head and sighed. "Your mother always was a wild one. She had a way of drawing trouble to her like a light draws the moth. Those two fighting mongrels both thought they owned your mother."

Vandre swallowed. "Owned?"

"Like a man owns a beast. The trouble is your mother never belonged to anyone... except maybe you."

He shook his head. "But how did it all begin?"

The old woman sighed. "The one doing all the beating said your mother was his. He came to her wagon tonight and she told him no. When he wouldn't leave, the one receiving the beating came to her defense. He said your mother and he were bound, and the other fellow had no place with her. The big fellow took to arguing, attacked your mother and she fought back like a cornered cat. He did not approve of that and ran her through with a knife. That was all the other man needed to attack. The skirmish knocked over lanterns and disrupted fires, hence the current situation we are in now."

Vandre's mind was all in a haze. "I don't understand. My mother has never bound herself to anyone."

"True. But he did say some truth. I know I speak out of turn, but that man losing to the behemoth is your father."

Now Vandre felt blackness creeping over his mind. He was spinning. His father. "My father never made himself known. I... I thought he was a figment of the past." He looked through the wheels of the wagon. The man now known to him as his father lay face down in the dirt, with the man known as his parent's attacker on top of him, squeezing the life out of his father's body.

His father.

Vandre leaped to his feet and plunged under the wagon. He lunged at the large man, knocking him sideways to the ground. An animalistic rage possessed him, and he hit the man, blow after blow squarely in the face. He heard the crowd roar in surprise. A voice shouted in his ear, "Enough!" and he felt strong arms pull him back. He shook the arms off and rushed to the man, now known to him as his father. Gently he turned him over. There was no life left in his soulless eyes. He cradled his head and pulled the lifeless body to his chest. This was how he was to meet his father. *This?*

Another man approached him. In his arms, he bore Vandre's mother. Her hands fell away from her wound, and her eyes stared through her son into the afterlife she had entered so very tragically and unexpectedly. The man lay her body next to that of her lover, her head resting on the knee of her son. He stood and gazed down at the boy and shook his head.

"This tribe no longer wants you here, boy. Your mother was trouble, and you are her mongrel pup. We want none of your trouble."

Vandre was numb, his body completely void of any possible response. The dying fires breathed smoke into his lungs and eyes and enveloped him in a thick cocoon. He heard the shouts to pull the wagons away and felt the ground tremble under the hooves of the horses and the groan of the wheels, but he was immovable in his sorrow.

The dust settled, the smoke dissipated, and Vandre was left alone. The silence was so immense he felt as though the whole world must have become quiet. Gently, he laid his parent's heads on the ground and stood. The gypsies had left the clearing in a disarray of burnt rubble and ruin. He shifted through smoldering piles of rubbish to find some means of digging. He found the blade of a shovel, its shaft burned to cinders. He pulled it from the rubbish and walked to the edge of the clearing. Falling to his knees, he struck the earth with the blade, willing it to part, to be wounded for the sake of his grief. He raised the blade again and again, striking the earth again and again. A blow for his mother—abused, neglected, and now, murdered. A blow for his father—a man he saw daily, yet who lied to him, who only became noble at the last moment of his selfish life. And blow after blow for himself—outcast and rejected son of no one.

He buried them together so that in the afterlife they would not be alone, he loved his mother too much to leave alone, even in death. He covered them with the smoke-scented earth, hiding their love once more. And then, he turned and walked away from the only thing that had ever felt familiar to him into the woods, dark and unknown, and yet somehow far more welcoming than any human had ever been.

He wandered for days, living off the berries and roots of the woods and water of the stream. He slept like a wild thing, huddled in the bracken-covered hollows abandoned by their previous dwellers. Gone were the voices of his imagination, gone was the magic of the Vale as he buried himself deep in the darkness of the forest. He felt himself lost to the world of man, lost to the world of knowledge, he had so desperately tried to enter. Slowly, he felt himself slip from being more man to becoming more beast.

And it was in this state that he came upon a long and winding path leading up the crest of a hill that seemed to climb into the mists. The road was paved, which in Vandre's mind, seemed strange for this part of the woods. As he climbed higher, lips in the stone began to jut out, creating what seemed to be steps. But these steps were a thing of a distant past, cracked and covered with the passage of time. He did not know where they led; he did not care. If it were to be a reprieve from his wanderings, so be it. If they led to some unforeseen death, he would welcome that too.

As he climbed, he began to be aware of the sensation that he was being watched. The hairs rose on the back of his neck as though someone were following his every move. He searched the edge of the trees but could see no movement. The mists curled about his feet and tricked his eyes with shadows. He dismissed his imagination and believed his mind to be playing tricks on him.

And then, the sound of footsteps rose from behind him. Or were they to his side? The mists rose and grew thicker almost as though the owner of the footstep had beckoned them. Vandre quickened his step and felt his body tense. There was no mistaking the sound of footfalls. His gaze darted all about, but there was no sign of anyone or anything, only the sound of footsteps. He turned to look behind him and the sound stopped. Vandre swallowed and backed up slowly.

"Be mindful of where you step, lad."

Vandre whirled around, tripping on the hem of his cloak and falling backward. His hands found the end of a stick and he gripped it tightly. Scrambling to his feet, he thrust the stick into the mists. "Who are you? What do you want?"

As if to answer him, the mists parted to reveal a figure hooded from head to toe in gray. He leaned heavily on a long black staff, and Vandre wondered why he had not heard the staff upon the path. He surmised that the figure was that of a man, though he could not see their face. Vandre brandished his stick, though he knew he must look like a fool. "I will ask you again, what is it you want? I have nothing to give you, I am an orphan traveling alone."

The figure removed their hood, and Vandre realized he had been correct. Before him stood the figure of a man, or at least, he thought him to be a man. He was tall, much taller than any man Vandre had ever met before. His hair was gray, yet he bore the visage of youth. In fact, his face looked as though it were carved from river stone, with perfectly etched features that framed two eyes that seemed to pierce Vandre from front to back. These eyes regarded Vandre with amusement as though they somehow had followed him his entire journey.

CHILD OF DAWN

Those eyes unsettled Vandre even more than he already was. He thrust the stick at the figure, who seemed to be amused by his tenacity. "I will ask you a third and final time…"

Before he could finish, he found his stick knocked from his hands and himself on his back, the figure's staff at his throat. The eyes that unsettled him were now inches from his face. "Perhaps it is I who should be asking *you* why you trespass."

Vandre pushed the staff away. "Trespass on ruins?" He stood and brushed himself off. "I fear your mine is addled, old man. The woods took charge of these lands long ago."

The figure smiled and Vandre felt as though he were being toyed with. "My master owns these woods, this road, and the air around it."

Vandre scoffed. "No one can own air."

The figure's eyes narrowed. "Take care what you say, boy. The master is listening." He turned and peered into the woods. "The master has eyes and ears everywhere." He turned back to Vandre. "Now, the way I see it, you have two options. You can either continue to wander about like a lost lamb, or you can return to the castle with me, where a hot meal awaits."

"Castle?" Vandre looked about. "There is no castle in these woods. You must think me a fool to follow you. I do not even know your name."

The figure raised an eyebrow. "Nor I yours." He bowed slightly. "But I have manners. I am Gammel, keeper of Castle Skog."

Vandre was now convinced the forest was listening. At the mention of the castle, the mists cleared, and a great castle rose out of the ground. It seemed to be built into the rocky earth itself and rose up against mountainous cliffs that could only be seen on a clear day. To Vandre, it seemed as though both building and earth cohabitated the space in some sort of symbiotic harmony. For he could not tell where the building ended, and the earth began.

He stood in awe at this revelation before him. Finding his voice, he asked, "Who is your master?"

Gammel smiled. "Where are *your* manners, boy? You have yet to tell me your name. And your purpose here."

Vandre lowered his eyes back to the face with inquisitive eyes. "My name is Vandre. And I have no purpose."

Gammel smiled. "Everyone has a purpose. And there is meaning in everything one does."

Vandre shrugged. "You know nothing of my life, old man."

Gammel's smile turned to laughter. "Nothing? Nothing of your conversations with creatures on the other side of the Vale? Nothing of your desire for knowledge?" His voice softened. "Nothing of your loss?"

Vandre shrank back. "You have been watching me? Why? What am I to you?"

Gammel leaned against his staff. "You have spoken to the Vale. We can always hear voices that search us out."

Vandre was uncertain he wanted clarification. "We?"

Gammel pulled his hair away from the sides of his face to reveal two ears that curved and then met in a pointed tip. "I am not of this world, Vandre of the wood. I am an elf."

Vandre gasped. "But how…"

The elf raised his hand. "It is a story longer than your journey. And you have completely diverted me. Yes, boy, I have watched you. I have heard you. And now I am offering you food and lodgings. I have need of someone to help me, an apprentice. For while my master needs me, I need someone to aid in my own work."

"And what is your work?"

"So many questions for someone lacking the need for answers!" He offered Vandre his hand. "Do you want a meal in your belly or not?"

Vandre was uncertain as to whether this creature from another world had swayed some sort of power over him, or his own body wracked with hunger had taken possession of his tongue. "A meal would be most welcome."

Gammel struck his staff against the stone. "Excellent!" He set off up the road, moving far quicker than Vandre thought an old man should. "Keep up, boy. Getting lost in these woods would not bode well for you."

Vandre could not help but wonder if having been found by this elf was the best thing for him.

Vandre continued to live with this uncertainty for the next several years, though it dimmed with each passing meal and each night spent with a roof over his head. Castle Skog proved to be as formidable up close as it was amongst the mists. It creaked and groaned with story and mystery, speaking to those who trespassed upon its thresholds. Vandre indeed felt as though he was a trespasser, despite living there and working as Gammel's apprentice. he could not shake the sense that the castle did not welcome him. It seemed to possess a soul of its own—it lived and breathed with the mountain. When he walked thro·

dimly lit corridors it seemed to creak a continuous complaint from wall to hearth.

He soon found out that working with Gammel meant performing any and every task the elf asked him to do. At best, he worked with Gammel in his shop mixing all manner of herbs and mysterious compounds. At worst, he was Gammel's lackey—sent to do menial errands in the woods. Vandre thought this was strange for three reasons. The first being that Gammel always warned him of the danger of the woods, and yet he was continuously sent out into them in search of some plant or to hunt for food. The second reason being that he was always ordered to do this at night. Vandre thought this made it particularly ridiculous, but Gammel argued that often the forest shifted in the moonlight and therefore things were easier to find. Vandre thought this to be absurd. The final reason was that, even though Gammel always told him it was the master of the castle who wished him to go, Vandre never was told by the master himself.

In fact, Vandre had never seen the master whom he supposedly served.

There was little evidence there was anyone else even living in the castle. Vandre questioned Gammel's sanity at times and wondered if the elf was completely mad and they were alone. But small signs would appear every so often. A footprint etched in the dust and too large to be Gammel's, a chair moved, curtains closed when Vandre was certain he had opened them. Often when he lay in his bed, he would hear voices through the rafters high overhead, though he always convinced himself he was dreaming. Shadows would cross his path but appear to have no owner, and he would often feel a breeze against his face when the wind was silent.

He pestered Gammel with questions, but he never received direct answers. The elf would often speak in riddles or indirect responses. There was always some valid reason the master was not seen. Vandre tried to find a painting or sketch of the man who seemingly had complete control of his life, but there were none. With the passage of time, Vandre came to believe that his master either be a monster or a complete myth.

One day, as the twilight approached over the western hills, Gammel called for Vandre and told him to find a plant known as foxberry. It grew at the edge of the forest, near meadows at the base of the mountains. Vandre groaned, knowing the long trek that lay before him. But he had learned not to argue and so threw his cloak about his shoulders and set off with a satchel slung over his shoulders.

He had come to know the path that brought him to Castle Skog almost by memory. The darkness and mists no longer thwarted him, nor did he fear what lay in the shadows. He knew each bend, each crack in the stone. The cries of the nightingale no longer caused him to jump, nor did the growl of the wolf. For he had come to understand that as a dweller of the castle he was protected by some unforeseen force that kept all harm at bay.

As he descended to the flatlands, the sounds of civilization returned to his ears. He could hear the tinkling of sheep bells and the lowing of cows in their stables. He heard the clinking of metal and chopping of wood, the squeak of wheels against the road, and the distant bark of a solitary dog. Vandre thought of the gypsies and the life he had lived before Gammel and his life in the castle and he was struck with the realization that he did not miss it all.

Crossing from the stone road into the meadow, he looked for the foxberry Gammel had tasked him with finding. It was a dark green plant with deep purple buds. Of its purpose he was unsure, but he knew that the elf used it in whatever potions he concocted. He found some creeping out from underneath a large boulder. Kneeling, he gently began to pull it up in small bunches.

As he worked, he heard people walking the road. Not wishing to be seen and give an introduction, he leaned into the cool surface of the rock and listened as they approached. They were all men with boisterous voices raised in a heated conversation. Peeking around the corner of the rock, he noticed that they all carried various bits of farming tools but were brandishing them more as weapons and less as the means by which to carry out their daily chores.

One of the men sliced at the tall grasses with his scythe as he stomped by Vandre's hiding place. "Tonight, it ends!" The others roared in agreement. "Years of mist and misery. No more! It ends with Anda!"

The men screamed themselves into a frenzy. "Ends with Anda! Ends with Anda!" they yelled as they thrust their weapons and fists into the air and marched off into the mists.

Vandre crept out from behind the stones and shoved the foxberry into his satchel. The mist curled around his feet in gray wisps and pulled him back toward the woods. The wind swept down from the mountains and lightning snapped across the sky. Vandre gripped his cloak tightly about him as all manner of weather whipped around him. He crashed into the forest as the heavens opened and poured down rain. In the storm, he could see nothing. Water cascaded off dripping leaves and flew into his eyes with the force of the wind. Branches clutched at his cloak and scratched his skin through his clothes. He yanked at the hem of his cloak, twisting with force, and catching his foot on an upturned root.

He felt his feet leave the ground. He tumbled backward, his body crashing into something immovable, before falling to the earth. He lay there stunned, gazing up at the wet heavens. The earth beneath him shifted and he rolled over to gaze into the face of a girl.

Chapter 3

Her anger enveloped her. *Witch.* So that was what she was to them.

Someone who boiled spells in a cauldron and cackled in the dark of the night. Someone who turned foolish boys into toads and gave selfish girls warts on their noses. Her tears burned her face as they cascaded down her cheeks. The wind wrapped her cloak like a cocoon around her and pulled her into the darkness of the forest—the pounding sound of the label branded on her soul... *Witch... Witch...* echoing in her head.

She stumbled blindly over uprooted branches that nipped at her heels. The wind lifted the leaves from the ground and hurled them about in an aerial whirlpool of chaos. They smacked into her face and arms, smearing her with grime and then passing on into the darkness. Her rage equaled her sheer terror in knowing how despised she was. And for what? The elements? The misfortunes of others? How could the village blame her for something that was so completely beyond her control?

Anda stepped out into the air and felt herself fall for what seemed like an endless eternity, only to crash into the earth and tumble through the mud down the face of a steep heel. She slid to a stop in the hollow at the base of a tree. She pulled her knees to her chest and nestled herself in the crook of the roots of the tree. There was no more going on, no more willing herself to survive. What was the point when everyone thought her to be a monster? She would let nature take her. Her body would dissolve into the earth, and no one would ever be bothered by her again.

But then the wind curled gently around her huddled frame and Anda felt it gently pull her up. Maybe she was dreaming. She kept her eyes closed in the hopes that she would sink back into oblivion. But then, she heard something over the storm around her. A voice, faint, and seemingly distant, but familiar.

Anda.

She knew that voice somehow and yet could not associate to whom it belonged. It was like a memory, faded, but still present in the recesses of her mind.

Anda, get up.

Anda opened her eyes and pulled herself up. "Who are you?" she called out into the swirling mists.

I am your mother. You must not give up, Anda. You have so much more to give.

She stumbled forward. "Mother? Where are you?"

You have only to look within to find me, and to know yourself.

"Mother!" Anda screamed. The wind picked up and pushed her forward into the mists. It shrieked and howled. Anda matched its cries with her own, groping wildly in the hopes she would find herself in her mother's embrace.

Suddenly, her body crashed into a seemingly immovable object, and she found herself falling backward. Her back and head thudded into the earth as something crushed down on her, pressing her further into the ground. The mists lifted and she found herself gazing into the wide eyes of a young man. His mouth hung open in shock and he stared down at her like a frightened animal.

Anda's eyes narrowed. "Remove yourself," she hissed through clenched teeth.

The young man scrambled backward and offered his hand. "My apologies. I did not see you there." He moved closer, his hand still extended. "I do not bite. Please, let me help you."

Anda took his hand and he pulled her to her feet. "You are a fool to be out here in weather such as this," she grumbled as she fumbled with her hair.

The young man laughed and reached up to pull a leaf from her tousled hair. "You might say the same for yourself."

"I know these woods!" Her eyes flashed. "Take care to not insult the person you just knocked to the ground."

"Forgive the correction, but you crashed into me."

Anda looked at him for a moment, completely flustered at his calmness. She straightened her skirt and arched an eyebrow. "Well, who was on top of whom?"

The young man bowed slightly. "Again, my apologies." He removed his cloak and swung it around her shoulders. "Now, if I am to be polite, and well-behaved, might I know for whom I am exhibiting good behavior?"

Anda fumbled with the clasp of the cloak. "My name is Anda." She looked down at the clasp. "And thank you for the cloak."

He smiled. "It is my pleasure." Anda turned and began walking away. Vandre hastened to stop her. "Might you wish to know my name?"

Anda sighed. "It had not crossed my mind, no."

It did not deter him. "Vandre. My name is Vandre. It means, 'to wander.'"

"It's wonderful to see you are living up to your name's expectations."

He laughed. "Oh, I am not wandering anymore. I used to. My people were gypsies." He paused briefly and Anda noticed his face cloud over briefly with sadness. "But they are gone, and I have a new master with a home not far from here."

Anda stopped. "You live nearby?" She pulled her cloak about her and thought of the warmth of a fire and how good food would be to eat.

Vandre realized he had said too much. "I do. But my master does not take kindly to guests. In fact, I do not think he takes kindly to anyone."

Anda raised an eyebrow. "And why is that?"

"In truth, I have never seen him."

Anda laughed. "You are joking."

Vandre shook his head. "Not one bit."

"Then how do you even know he is your master?"

"His servant brought me to his home. I was abandoned by my people, and he found me wandering in the woods. I had nowhere else to go, so I followed him home. In truth, I work more for this old man, than the master. But I know the master is there. I hear him."

"You *hear* him?"

"It seems he favors the night. I will hear him walking on the upper floors. There will be footprints in the hallways and things will be moved ever so slightly from where I left them. In truth, there are times I wonder if he is some sort of magical creature."

"Why would you think that?"

"Because the man who found me is. In fact, he is no man. He is an elf."

Anda froze. "An elf?"

Vandre laughed. "Oh, he is harmless. At least, most days he is. He can be irritable at times. He is not like other elves."

Anda's eyes narrowed. "What do you mean, *other* elves?"

He shrugged. "Oh, temperamental, flying into a fit of passion every time someone angers or offends them. Using magic to control the will of others. Those elves."

Anda's blood seethed within her. Her mind tumbled like an unsettled sea. This pebble of a man was insulting her mother, insulting *her*. And he was too pathetic to even realize it. The wind that had subsided now whipped up once more into a raging flurry. Branches snapped at their faces and the mists swirled about them.

A branch crashed to the earth behind Vandre. He reached for Anda's hand, but she pulled away. "Do not touch me!" she screamed.

He was taken aback by her response but persisted. "We must get inside! This storm will be the death of us!"

Anda stepped backward. She could feel the electricity coursing through her veins, making every inch of her pulse with rage. She did not know where the rage came from, nor how to extinguish the fire that raged within her. Her body boiled in a white-hot flame despite the chilled wind that swept around her. She was as frightened of herself as she was certain Vandre was of her.

She turned to flee but was stopped by some invisible force. There appeared to be nothing in front of her, and yet, she could not move forward. She raised a hand to push against what looked to be only air but could not move it past the edge of her face. And then, the space around her shifted, like a ripple in a reflection when disturbed by a fallen leaf. She pushed against the invisible wall and things began to transfigure. What was once a birch tree was now an oak, fuzzy and muted in color, like a disturbed watercolor, but a tree entirely changed in appearance. The ground became water, the cloudy sky became clear and filled with starlight. She pushed her hand harder against the unseen force and things became clearer. She could feel her body shake as though it would shatter but was blissfully aware that she did not care.

And then, she was wrenched back into her world of solid, singular colors. She gasped for air, not realizing she had ceased to breathe. Vandre was gripping her arm tightly, his eyes wide and his fingers digging into her flesh. The air stilled itself, and the forest fell silent so that all could be heard was the cadence of their breathing.

"What..." Vandre could not form words on his tongue. "What was that?"

Anda tried to calm the fire boiling inside her. "I do not know what you mean."

Vandre pulled back. "Are you a witch?"

She bit her lip. "I have been called that."

"What did you do to the..."

"I cannot control it. I do not know how. In fact, I do not even know what *it* is."

"You possess the Valen magic. You can split the wall between this world and the world of magic. The elf of whom I spoke told me of this power. But only elves possess it. So that would make you..."

"An elf? Anda turned away. "An outcast? A pariah?"

Vandre's tone softened. "Those words never crossed my mind."

"My mother was an elf. My father is a human. A farmer and a good man. I inherited my mother's magic, my sister did not. I was driven from my home; my sister now runs the farm with her husband. So, I think "outcast" would be the perfect word to describe me."

Vandre smiled. "Misunderstood, maybe. Not outcast. And most certainly gifted."

Anda realized that his kind words were unfamiliar to her. She shifted uncomfortably from one foot to the other. "I do not even know how I do it. I do not even know *if* it is me that causes it. The village I came from blamed me for a mist that would not leave. I did not call it, nor conjure it. Yet still I was blamed." A lump rose in her throat. "And now I am wandering through the woods, cold, hungry, and alone.

"Well," Vandre slung his bag over his shoulder. "That, I can help with." He offered her his hand and when she did not take it, he laughed. "I know, I know. I would be wary of strangers as well. Except you are the one who just shifted the world around us, so I should be the one who is uneasy. Now, I can offer you a hot meal and perhaps someone who will have answers for you."

Anda remained suspicious, but the promise of a hot meal outweighed any sort of fear she had. She took his hand and followed him up the path, deep into the unknown of the forest and own existence.

Castle Skog was nothing like Anda imagined it would be. The sheer immensity of the castle, the way it jutted out of the mountainside, and still seemed completely assimilated into the surrounding landscape both overwhelmed and enthralled her. It was as though the very rocks it sat upon had breathed it into existence. Each path, each buttress, every arch seemed a part of the earth from which it rose. The moss and ivy mingled with stone and iron, intermingled in a flawless medley of architecture. Indeed, Anda could not clearly see where the castle ended, and the heavens began. The place was cloaked in a heavy stillness with no sound but the occasional drip of water falling from a hanging eave to the cold crevice between cobblestones.

Vandre led her under the arch, now more fauna than stone. A deep canyon separated three sides of the castle from the rest of the forest, connected only by a wooden bridge. The rear of the castle was flanked by the mountains rising in an impenetrable shield as far as the eyes could see. Water cut through the canyon below, smooth and silent as it flowed over a sandy river bottom and smooth rocks, long ago worn down by the river's force.

The bridge led to a stony outcropping on which two trees, gnarled with age, sat. They were void of any foliage, but their roots and branches twisted together in intricate patterns, creating art from their barren state. At the base of each tree sat a sentient statue of what Anda assumed were elves, so chiseled and perfect were their features. One statue depicted a warrior leaping into battle, sword raised and ready to strike some invisible enemy. Their hair streamed behind them in stony wisps. The other statue depicted a female elf, every detail of her face perfectly crafted. Her hands were open, offering up unspoken wonders to those who passed by. As Anda walked under them she was aware that she was passing from one realm into another, and this new place was full of magic so powerful it drew her breath from her body and filled it instead with a desire she did not understand.

Vandre led her up steps split by wandering roots and covered in moss dripped in dew. The rushing of the river grew distant the higher they climbed. Mist cascaded down from the turrets and parapets, its long tendril-like wisps wrapped around Anda's body, pulling her ever upward. She was entranced by the haunting beauty of the place. It was as though an unseen mage had cast a spell over everything, suspending it within its own time and place.

Vandre glanced sideways at her and laughed. "You look like a child watching stars fall."

Anda shut her mouth she knew had slipped open in wonderment. "I don't look like anything of the sort," she retorted. "Places like this don't exist in the real world."

He laughed again. "This *is* the real world." He helped her over a stray boulder. "The world just forgot about it."

Anda reached out and ran her hand over an old stone wall. Ivy crept along the cracked surface, and moss peeked out from the crevices. "The air is heavy," she whispered. "Old. Like everything around us is holding its breath."

Vandre led her across a courtyard and pushed open a door that looked even older than its surroundings. It creaked and groaned, and a rush of air rolled out with a sigh. Vandre leaned against the door and offered her his hand. "Welcome to the oldest part of this place. The workshop."

Anda stepped into the room, ignoring the hand Vandre offered her. She knew her mouth was gapping again, and she did not care. It wrapped her in bewitchment. The walls were lined with bottles and decanters filled with a myriad of colorful concoctions. They caught the stray rays of sunlight and cast rainbows up to the rafters. Dried plants and flowers tied with twine hung in bunches, sending down their fragrances in waves. But what caught Anda's eye was the table in the middle of the room. It was long and rectangular and was covered with old pieces of parchment. Upon these was a language completely indiscernible to her, and maps of locations she did not recognize. The smell of old parchment mixed with the dried plants above her created a wonderfully overwhelming aroma and made her feel as though she were floating.

"They are mesmerizing, are they not?" Vandre picked up one of the parchments.

Anda swallowed. "I do not recognize the text."

Vandre smiled. "Do you not recognize your own language? It is elvish. Though from what Gammel says, it is an ancient dialect."

"Elvish?" Anda studied a parchment covered in sketches of some mythical creature who looked to be half man, half bird. "Why would an old man be studying elvish?"

"Because that old man is an old elf."

The door creaked further open, and they both turned to see a hooded figure standing in its frame. The figure let the hood fall to their shoulders to reveal the graying face of a man. His eyes glistened and were both merry and piercing. Lines trickled down his face in rivulets to the corners of pursed lips. He leaned heavily on his tall staff, gripping it tightly with two gnarled hands.

Anda was unsure if he was happy to see her or enraged at her presence. She swallowed the ever-growing lump in her throat and did the only thing she could think to do. She gathered her skirt above her ankles and sank into a low curtsy, lowering her eyes to study the bits of dirt on the floor. When silence remained in the room, she tilted her head to look back up at the man.

He pushed himself up on his staff and took a step closer. "I may appear old to the human's ignorant eye, but for an elf… I am quite young."

Anda lowered her eyes once more. "Forgive me, my lord. I made no assumptions about your age."

The pursed lips slowly parted, and the eyes grew brighter. A laugh ruptured from his wizened frame, and he offered Anda his hand. "Wise words, young one. Never judge someone by the wrinkles on their skin!"

Vandre seemed to be relieved at the turn of events. "Anda, this is Gammel. Resident elf, apothecary, mage, and all manner of things mystic. And the person who tells me what to do."

Gammel struck Vandre across the shoulders. "And who has tried without success to teach you some respect!" He bowed slightly in Anda's direction. "It is an honor." He reached for her hand and gently lifted it to his lips. As his lips touched the surface of her skin, Anda felt a burst of energy ripple through her hand and up her arm. The shock from this caused her to jerk backward into the table and pull her hand away.

Gammel's eyes widened. He reached for her hand again and turned it palm upward. Pulling it close to his face, he studied it as though looking for something. He muttered something and then let her hand fall. "You are an elf!"

"Part elf," Vandre spoke up.

"Were you asked?" Gammel glared at him and Vandre stepped backward.

"He is right," Anda said, rubbing her hand. "I am only half elf.

Gammel studied her face. "Your father?"

She shook her head. "My mother."

"Indeed?"

"She fell through the Vale one stormy night and my father found her. She never went back."

"She lived here amongst man?"

"Until her death." Anda's eyes fell. "She died giving birth to me."

Gammel's gaze softened. "My child, she did this world a great service. Until today I believed myself to be the only one living within your world. And I must confess, it has not been by choice. But I am here, and too old as Vandre says, to do anything about returning home. And so, I stay."

Anda looked around. "It is a quite...*interesting* place."

Gammel laughed. "Forgive me, child. Where are my manners? If Vandre dragged you up here, it must be because you are hungry."

"Hungry, cold, tired, lost, and alone."

"Gammel led her out into the courtyard. "Then you have come to the right place. We are all outsiders here, but we have food." He turned to Vandre. "Bring bread and cheese and find some wine."

Vandre looked perplexed. "Wine? But the master does not drink wine…"

Gammel's eyes narrowed. "Use the intelligence that prompted you to bring this poor girl all the way up here to find some!" As Vandre scurried off, he turned back to Anda. "Please," he gestured toward a pile of stones that had once been a bench. "Come sit by me." Anda complied and he turned toward her as if to study her. "There is an air about you, lass. A sense of conflict. As though your very body was at war with itself. Tell me, did your mother leave you any of her gifts?"

Anda blinked. "Her gifts?"

"Did she possess any special, how should I put this?"

"He means did your mother have any magical powers?" Vandre placed a small platter of food next to Anda.

Gammel looked at him with furrowed eyebrows. "I don't recall you being in this conversation, boy."

Vandre smiled. "Just translating for you." He crossed to a well that stood not far off. Dipping a wooden ladle into the bucket that rested on the ledge, he walked back and offered it to Anda. "Here," he said. "You will find water this sweet nowhere else."

Gammel sighed. "I was specific in saying bring wine."

"And I was specific in saying there is no wine anywhere. We both know it is not to the master's liking."

Anda took the ladle and held it to her lips. The water was indeed sweet. It smelled of flowers and rain-drenched leaves. There was a cold sharpness that pricked at her tongue as she swallowed it. "Indeed, Vandre is correct. This water tastes wonderful."

Gammel's eyes narrowed. "To each their own liking, I suppose."

Anda reached for the bread and shoved a piece in her mouth. She had not realized how hungry she was. Gammel and Vandre smiled bemusedly as they watched. She noticed their gaze blushed. "Forgive me. My manners seem to have left me."

"Nonsense!" Gammel waved his hand. "Eat, and we will let you rest before you are on your way."

She swallowed. "Oh. Must I leave today?"

"Could she not stay longer?" Vandre inquired. "She could have my room. I can sleep in the stables."

Gammel lowered his voice. "Would you have the master find her here?"

"The master will not even know she is here. Indeed, he never stirs until the night. And she will be safely in bed by then."

"As much as I would be fascinated to speak with someone who shares the same blood as I, it would be foolish for her to linger. Think what the master would do if he found her here."

"But she would be hidden," Vandre protested.

"Do you think he would not sense her presence?" Gammel lifted his eyes to the skies. "As he may even now sense it."

Anda set her bread back down on the tray. "Just exactly what sort of man is this master you speak of? He sounds ominous."

Gammel was quick to respond. "Not ominous. Mysterious perhaps. He is a creature of the night."

"An invisible creature," Vandre muttered under his breath.

"Silence!" Gammel snapped. "Do you wish for him to hear your mutterings?"

Vandre rolled his eyes. "Perhaps he does not even have ears. Perhaps he is more beast than man and possesses a forked tongue and tail. But how could we ever know for certain? He never shows himself to anyone but you!"

Anda stood. "I believe I have overstayed the little welcome I had. I shall be on my way and find shelter elsewhere." She curtsied slightly in Gammel's direction. "Thank you for your hospitality." Turning to Vandre she nodded and smirked, "And thank you for bumping into me in the woods."

Vandre gripped her hand. "I wish you would stay. The woods are dangerous."

Gammel stepped between them. "Castle Skog is equally perilous. You stand a far better chance out there." He placed his hand on her forehead. "There is strength in you, my child. Do not doubt yourself. You have power hidden within you. Power to change fate."

Anda's gaze remained locked with Gammel's. There was something in his eyes, something pulling her in. They drew her down into a swirling cosmos of mystery and memory, speaking to her in a tongue that both confused and calmed her. She was sinking and yet flying at the same time. She did not understand the secrets he was sharing, but her heart told her she was somehow connected to the magic, and she found herself longing to know more.

A piercing shriek cut through her thoughts and pulled her back to the present. She looked around, almost having forgotten where she was. She felt disoriented and detached from her surroundings. She heard Vandre's voice calling her name and saw him rushing toward her.

"Here," he whispered. "Take my cloak and be off. Gammel was right. You stand a better chance out in the woods." He threw his cloak on her shoulders and pushed her toward the steps that led down toward the water. "Go!"

Anda stumbled backward, half wondering why he was whispering. She heard the shriek again, this time louder and more pronounced. She clutched the cloak to her body and turned toward the steps. She could hear wind rushing overhead and a chill filled the air. Mist crept in over the cobblestone, snaking its saw around her ankles. The wind howled, but she felt no breeze on her face. Looking up, she saw that the clouds had darkened to an inky black, blocking out any remnants of the sun.

Something invisible rushed past her, brushing hard against her shoulders. She whirled about and saw Vandre gesturing wildly to flee. Gammel stood still, clutching his staff, and scanning the skies. Again, something whirled past her. This time she was certain she heard the sound of wings.

"Run!" Vandre screamed over the howling of the wind.

Anda took a step and caught her food on the hem of the cloak. Her body twisted as she fell, her head smashing into the stone wall. The world collided in sparks of colors fraying into blackness. Vandre's and Gammel's voices became distant, and then silent. A shadow crossed over her closed eyes, and she tilted her head involuntarily in its direction. The heavens opened and rain poured down drenching her to the skin. There was a softer rush of wind, and she sensed the shadows settle behind her. Bits of rock crumbled from the top of the wall and down into the cloak and against her neck.

With all her strength, she pushed her eyes open and turned her face to the top of the wall. Peering through heavy lids, she saw that she was being scrutinized by what appeared to be a man. He was crouched like a lion observing its prey, waiting to pounce. His head was tilted to one side, listening for something she could not hear. Anda's head pounded, and she could feel the blood rushing through her veins toward both her injured head and thudding heart. Through her daze, she observed that he wore no shoes and that his skin was pale white. *No,* she fought against her own thoughts. *White is the wrong word.* For it was more than just white. It was marbled. It shone like moonlight on a wheatfield. It was hard, smooth, and chiseled.

Her eyes fell shut with their own weight and she slipped into semi-consciousness wondering why she was so observant of this man's skin. She heard Gammel's voice, this time closer, and someone lifted her up and half-carried, half-dragged her for several feet.

"My Lord," it was Gammel's voice. Anda could hear apprehension under his even tone. "She was in the woods. Vandre did not think you would be home for several hours. Indeed, Vandre did not think at all."

"Forgive me, my lord."

Anda envisioned Vandre groveling.

"I will take her to the forest's edge. She will be of no further nuisance." Anda felt a gentle tug on her arm.

She was immediately wrenched back, her back dragged across small bits of rock, cutting through her clothes. But her head was too heavy for her to care.

"You will not hurt her, my lord." Gammel's voice raised ever so slightly, but still quivered. "She is of your mother's race."

A shadow passed over Anda's face and she could hear snarling and growling, as though surrounded by wild dogs. In the distance, she could hear wolves howling and she shivered.

The wind screamed over the walls and through the crevices and a loud crack splintered Anda's head. "Nó harnalë!"[1] Gammel's voice roared.

She felt her body fall away from the earth and her body bent in half, her arms falling over her head. She was rising and the cold air stung her face, reviving her consciousness. She was aware of the rush of wings and a firm grip around her waist. Droplets of water crashed against eyelids and their frigid temperature stung them. She turned her head and saw the castle wall falling away beneath her.

And then, the air warmed ever so slightly, and she felt herself settled to the ground. She heard whispering in the shadows and then the voices of women moaning. A door groaned open and crawled shut as though never to open again. Padded footsteps by her head mingled with hurried ones outside the door.

Anda was through being dazed. She pushed herself halfway up and leaned back on her elbows. The room was dark and

---

[1] Nó harnalë means "no harm" in Elvish.

filled with shadows. There were no furnishings, no signs of life or living anywhere.

Suddenly there was pounding on the door. "Anda!" It was Vandre's voice.

The door burst open and Vandre tumbled into the room with Gammel close behind.

"Are you all right?" Gammel knelt beside her.

"Yes," I think so.

Vandre rushed to the window. "He is nowhere in sight."

Gammel grew very still. His eyes narrowed to focus on a seemingly blank bit of stone wall. "That is because he is hidden in shadow."

Anda looked up at Gammel and then followed his gaze. "Who? Who is?"

Gammel gripped her shoulder. "Anda, this is the master of Castle Skog."

The shadows shifted like rain clouds moving in the wind. Two eyes appeared, glinting and hard like flint. The outline of what appeared to be a human materialized from the darkness and moved toward them.

Slowly, Anda's memory came back to her. The man with the marble skin. The wings... the flying...

"Anda," Gammel's voice quivered. "This is Dagsbrún."

Chapter 4

Anda felt all breath leave her body and her knees buckle. Vandre caught her and eased her into a chair that seemingly materialized out of nowhere. This man, for she could call him nothing else, towered above her rising at least six feet above the ground. His skin which had first caught her attention below in the courtyard was translucent, opaque, and glowed with a dew-like sheen. The skin was stretched taut across a frame built like an oak, stitched together with sinewy veins that she could see ripple like water over his arms and up his neck.

He wore a waistcoat with tails over breeches, but no shirt, and his feet bare. His hair hung wild about his shoulders and was black like the ebony of the darkest wood. Tendrils of silver crept amongst the black locks like a river through a dark valley. His lips were pale, almost white, but full and wet, and slightly parted to slightly reveal proportioned teeth.

But his eyes, his eyes were his vortex. The irises were not inert but swirled about as though the very galaxies of the universe converged upon his face. They were at one moment the icy blue of a mountain spring, then the next the dewy green of a meadow at dawn. The very next moment, these two colors would collide across the pupil and create a kaleidoscope of color. Anda was fixed on them, her consciousness drawn from her body toward those orbs, yet her body paralyzed against her chair.

There was something within them, something so intoxicating, so frighteningly powerful that she felt herself drowning on dry ground.

Gammel spoke once more, and those eyes were shattered. "My lord, it is customary to greet guests."

The host did not move.

Gammel cleared his throat. "Generally, it is considered polite."

The man issued a low, guttural growl and Anda shrank back in her chair.

"My lord," Gammel stepped in front of Anda. "A bit of decorum, please. She is our guest."

"Guest!" There was a loud rush of wind. "There was no invitation issued!" He leaped across the room, knocking Gammel to the ground. Before she could breathe in, his fingers were about her throat. She felt their icy grip curl around her neck and was aware of each finger as it gripped the tiny hairs on the back of her neck.

"My Lord, she is elfin!"

His face softened ever so slightly, and he pulled away as though to better inspect Anda. He grabbed a handful of her hair and pulled it away from her ear and then growled in disgust. "She is a *half*-elf."

Gammel pushed himself to his feet. "Half is better than none. And a half-and-half in this place makes a whole if you could simply learn to do simple mathematics, my lord."

"Stop with your riddles, Gammel, you know I despise them." He turned and looked again at Anda. "What is your name?"

Gammel interjected. "I believe I told you her name was…"

"I asked her, not you! You want me to speak to her, I am speaking. Let me speak!" He took a step toward Anda. "I asked you a question."

Anda swallowed. "Anda."

"Anda." He turned and walked back toward the window. "As you have been told by this babbling mage, I am called Dagsbrún."

"I know," she whispered softly. "I heard."

"Would you mind telling me, Anda, why a half-breed is in my castle, unannounced and uninvited?"

Vandre, who had been huddled in the corner, stepped forward. "Well, you see, Sir, Gammel sent me to the woods, as he does often. And I was walking about when she appears. Not knowing any better, I make her angry and she sets off all manner of the elements. I thought it best she met Gammel since they both are elves, so I brought her here."

Anda thought Dagsbrún looked at Vandre as though he were deciding whether to eat him as one would eat a piece of meat. Vandre swallowed and shrank back once more. Anda began to feel herself grow irritated with this man named Dagsbrún's bullying. "See here, I did not ask to come here. In fact, I did not even ask to stay. Your henchmen, or whatever you would deem call them are the ones who at first wanted me to stay, then go. When I tried to leave, I fell, and after that, it was all a bit blurry... I somehow ended up here, in this room. I was run out of my home for being different, even though I do not know why I am different, and now I am being asked why I am here, even though I never asked to come here. It appears I am no longer wanted here either, so if you will excuse me, I will take my leave."

She moved toward the door, but his form seemed to shift from the window to the doorway in a single, breathless movement. So swift was his movement that her body slammed into his. His nostrils flared and pupils widened, darkening out the colors in his eyes. She could smell time itself on the folds of his waistcoat. Hints of leather, and musk; the wetness of the earth and aroma of the sky before a storm. The smell of old paper and fresh ink—all the stories of all time coursing through the body barricading her exit.

"I did not grant your exit," he growled.

"I did not ask for it," she hissed back. She tried to push past him.

He snarled and pushed her against the door. "You will stay! No one leaves Castle Skog! No one!"

"My lord!" Gammel slammed his staff to the ground. "A little decorum, please?"

Dagsbrún stepped back and straightened his waistcoat. "You would honor me if you would be my guest for the *unforeseeable* future."

Anda looked at Gammel and then back at Dagsbrún. "Am I correct in assuming I have no choice in the matter?"

"None whatsoever." Dagsbrún stepped to one side and gestured down the corridor.

She sighed and followed him. Gammel and Vandre followed a short distance behind as though they were uncertain as to what they were supposed to do. Anda felt as though she were being swallowed whole by the gaping mouth of the castle. The corridor yawned and stretched out into the darkness. The floors creaked and groaned, and walls seemed to shift and change so that she was never sure if they were turning left or right. The adrenalin began to seep from her body, and she did not care whether she was a captive or not. She simply wanted to sleep.

In her wearied state, she thought she heard voices around her. Whispers. Haunting voices behind walls where there were seemingly no rooms. She fought with her mind, arguing that she was hungry and tired, and therefore she was simply imagining things. But then, she thought she heard the voices discussing *her*. The girl. The half-elf. The outsider. But it could not be. Because the voices simply *were not there*.

They approached the end of a long, paneled hallway. Dagsbrún unlocked a vast door covered in tapestries and stood to one side to let Anda in. Wearily she walked past him into the room. She was too tired to care about her surroundings. She could make out the shape of a bed in the middle of the room and moved toward it.

"Vandre will sleep outside your room tonight. If you require anything, you have only to call out."

Without another word, he slammed the door shut, leaving her in near darkness.

Anda found her way to the bed and fell onto it. As sleep overtook her, she thought to herself that this bed had not been slept in for quite some time, and wondered how long she herself would be a prisoner in it.

Dagsbrún shut the door, locked it, and raged back down the hallway. Gammel left Vandre with a warning to not let Anda out, nor anything else *in,* and followed after Dagsbrún. He knew that the master of Castle Skog would rage and that he would bear the brunt of that rage. The stupid boy had been a fool for bringing the girl to the castle.

But he had been right. And right, without perhaps even knowing what he had down.

Dagsbrún stormed down long winding stairs, covered with carpet, long since frayed and faded. He crossed a grand hall with vaulted ceilings into an anteroom. He slammed his hand into a chair and leaped onto a table, strewn with old bits of paper and rubbish. Like a wild beast, he crossed the length of the table and came to rest at the opposite end in front of a roaring fire built up in a stone hearth.

He hunched down and stared at the fire, his eyes narrowing to small slits on his face. "Why do we build these fires, Gammel? You know they do me no service."

"True, my lord." Gammel sat beside Dagsbrún on a wooden bench. "However, it does warm my bones and the boys. And whether you care to admit it or not, you do need us."

Dagsbrún scoffed. "Need to? For what? To commit bumbling acts such as those you did today? What were you thinking, bringing that poor, hapless thing here? First, you find Vandre, and you drag his gypsy hindquarters here. I accept that because he has proved helpful. But now this... this halfling."

Gammel twisted his staff in his gnarled hands. "And what exactly would you call yourself, Dagsbrún? Be careful how you characterize someone when you yourself seem to forget your own reflection."

Dagsbrún stretched his hand out toward the fire and held it open palm upward. A slender filament of flame left the hearth and crept its way toward his outstretched hand, moving like a snake. It circled once around his hand and then settled above his finger in a bright burst of light, touching his flesh, but not burning it.

"I do not forget who I am. I remember all my curses."

"Then you would do well not to play with fire."

Dagsbrún turned his hand slightly towards Gammel and the tiny ball of flame erupted from his palm toward the elf. Gammel moved his staff to deflect it and the flame burst into an array of sparks that settled into ash on the floor.

Dagsbrún smiled, his white teeth flashing. "Well played, your old magic still works."

"It's that old magic that saved you, boy," Gammel stood to his feet. "It's that old magic that can save you again. There is a darkness inside of you, but there is also a light. Arrogance killed your parents, Dagsbrún. Don't let it be the death of you. You can do so much, but not on your own." With that, he turned and left Dagsbrún with his thoughts.

Chapter 5

Whether her sleep was uninterrupted by chance, or because Vandre stood vigilant all night, Anda awoke the next morning feeling as refreshed as one could in her circumstance. She rolled to one side and unraveled herself from the bedding. It was musty and faded, but still warm. The light peeking in from between the drapes let her better view her surroundings.

The room was decorated, if one could use that term, with ornate pieces that Anda was quite sure she would get lost in. A large pair of chairs sat by an empty fire, and an immense wardrobe, void of any clothing, sat on the wall opposite the bed. To the side of the wardrobe, there was a looking glass propped against the wall. Several tapestries hung on the wall, though they were faded, and it was difficult to see what they depicted. Anda felt as though they told stories that were not of this time, nor even of this world. She glimpsed violet eyes and horns atop human heads. Wild depictions of battles between man and beast tossing one another across starry expanses.

There was a knock at the door.

"Yes?"

The door creaked open and Vandre peeked around the edge. "Good morning."

Anda sat up. "Hello."

"Did you sleep well?"

"The point is, I slept."

"That is a fair point." Vandre closed the door and crossed the room to the window. He pushed the drapes open, flooding the room with light.

Anda scowled as the light hit her face and she put her hand up to shield her eyes.

Vandre smirked. "You do not like the sun either? You and the master will become great companions."

Anda threw her covers off and swung her feet over the side. "I do not mind the sun, except when I have slept little and dreamt much." As she placed her feet on the ground, she caught her reflection in the mirror. Her hair was matted and unkempt, and her clothes were dirty and torn. Smudges of dirt traced her face and hands. Had she become such a ragamuffin overnight? Of course, when was the last time she had seen her reflection? Perhaps she had looked this forlorn for quite some time and had had no knowledge of it.

Vandre saw her studying at herself and felt a twinge of guilt. It was partly his fault that she had fallen into this predicament. He crossed back to the door and cracked it open. The hallway was empty. Shutting the door, he rushed across the room and pushed the mirror to one side.

"What on earth..." Anda stumbled backward.

Vandre fell in the cracks between the stones. "The marvelous thing about earth-crumbling places like this is that they have stories built into them. And stories always come with a bit of excitement." He pushed a crumbling bit of mortar between the stones and a section of the wall receded to reveal a set of spiral stairs, leading downward.

Anda lunged for the archway. "An escape!"

Vandre stopped her. "Not an escape. There is no chance of that. He will hunt you and find you. And this time, he will not be so gracious."

Anda scoffed. "He will not find me. I will run."

Vandre lowered his voice. "He knows your scent, Anda. He will track you the same way you would track a rabbit for stew."

She swallowed and fought back her tears. "Then why show me this at all?"

"If you trust me, I will show you something that might make you feel a bit better."

Anda was uncertain as to whether Vandre could truly do anything to better her outlook on her current predicament. On the other hand, what did she have to lose? "I suppose even your worst would be an improvement. Lead on."

Vandre smiled, turned, and led her down the stairs. Their footsteps echoed and bounced against the walls, causing bits of rock to crumble to the ground. While dim, the stairs were not completely dark, which caused Anda to believe there must be an opening at the bottom. She touched the wall and a large stone crashed to the floor in front of her.

"Careful," Vandre warned. It does tend to crumble in places.

"How did you even know this was here?"

"Lord Dagsbrún keeps irregular hours. When I first came here, I had all the time in the world to explore this place. I know every secret about the castle."

"Do you know why your master is so odd?"

"Odd is not the word I would use to describe him."

Vandre paused on the stairs. "I would say irrational, enraged. Gammel would say tormented, conflicted. But Lord Dagsbrún is most certainly not odd. Just… different." He looked at Anda. "You should understand that. We both should."

Anda studied her feet. "I do not lock people away with no explanation."

Vandre continued down the steps. "True, but he has his reasons to trust no one. In time, perhaps you will come to understand."

"I think that highly unlikely."

Vandre laughed. "You find yourself very untrusting of yourself. As do I. We make an excellent band of misfits."

"I am banded to no one," she muttered under her breath.

A rush of cool wind hit her face as they came around the curve of the stairs. A doorway at the bottom opened to the outside. Cool green grass bejeweled with the morning dew met the stone floor of the castle as though the two were symbiotic. Anda placed her foot tentatively on the grass, half expecting to be swept back into the castle. The grass soothing on her bare feet and as her soles sunk into the earth, the green blades reached up and wrapped their verdant fingers around her toes.

Overhead the trees danced in a wondrous and tangled web. Their branches wove and worked together in a beautiful white and green tapestry that created a wispy canopy, permitting just the right amount of morning light. This light, though only allowed on the forest floor with permission, danced with the shadows as though it were there of its own accord. The shadow chased the light, and the light hid, only to rush out and scare the shadow back under a rock. And all this merriment created a glorious myriad of shapes and patterns on the comforting grass.

Anda was mesmerized by the ethereal scene before. As though she had once more been transported to yet another world. How could such beauty exist so close to a place of such darkness? She turned to Vandre who was watching her with a bemused look on his face. He gestured for her to follow him.

He laughed an almost childlike laugh and ran into a hollow of trees. Long willow branches hid the entrance, and she rushed to keep up with him. She pushed her way through, following his footsteps. As she made her way out, she saw another fantastical sight. There, amongst the wispy trees was a pool. Surrounded by smooth rocks of a gray and green hue, it twinkled in dim light. At the far end, the water disappeared into a small cave, draped at its mouth by a small waterfall. She crept closer, and though she could not be certain, she thought that as the water moved with the breeze it almost sounded as though its ripples made music—like the tinkling of a bell in the breeze. And when the water changed direction, so did the tone of the sound so that the water seemed to be serenading her with a whole symphony of sound.

"It is the Solv Pond." Vandre threw a pebble in the middle and the waters sparkled and the soft lilting sound rose to an operatic crescendo. "It sings of the forest, of its mysteries, its secrets."

"It is beautiful," Anda whispered.

"I thought perhaps you would like to bathe."

Anda stared at him incredulously. "Can one do that?" She looked back at the water. "It looks...as though one should not bathe in it. The waters seem too...virtuous."

Vandre laughed. "One thing you must learn, Anda, is that there is nothing virtuous about this pond, or forest, or anything within miles of this place. Appearances are always deceiving. No matter how beautiful, or hideous they are."

She was unsure if what he said made her feel any more at ease in this place. But the water looked both cool and cleansing and she could not remember the last time she had been able to bathe. "All right," she said. "But you must wait beyond the trees." Vandre looked at her with some confusion and she managed to smile. "This place may not be virtuous, but I still have some modesty. I'll not have you watching me bathe bare-skinned."

He held his hands up in surrender, bowed slightly, and walked back through the trees. "I am only on the other side if you need me."

"Thank you, I think I can manage a bath!"

He disappeared beyond the branches, and she turned back to the waters. She loosened the ties of her dress and let it and her chemise slip to the ground. Gingerly, she dipped her toes in the water. It was cool and bit at her feet, but not so frigid that it was unpleasant. She took a few steps more and then let all restraint slip away and dove down under the water. It caressed her skin like a sea of silk. The floor of the pond was filled with dancing grasses and delicate, white water flowers. Silvery pebbles caught strays of sunlight and twinkled like sunken starlight.

Anda raised her head to the surface. She could feel the dirt and grime fall away as rivulets of water cascaded down the sides of her face. She strode out of the water and reached for her clothes. As she slipped her chemise over her head, her ears pricked to rustling behind her. She turned back to the water but could see nothing.

"Vandre?" Her eyes scanned the perimeter of the clearing. "Vandre is that you?"

Instead of Vandre, another voice answered. "Why have you come to my home?"

Her eyes narrowed. "Who are you? Show yourself!"

The waters of the waterfall parted to reveal the figure of an immense black horse. Its mane and tail hung to the ground in silken black waves, and its hooves showed silver against the wet rocks. It looked at Anda briefly and then walked around the pond. Its eyes swam with various shades of browns and blacks, like fresh amber. "I will ask you again, why have you come to my home?"

Anda realized it was the horse who spoke. She blinked. The horse's mouth was not moving, but she knew it had spoked. "You can speak?"

The horse tossed its head. "Of course, I speak! I'll not ask you again. Why have you…"

"I was offered a bath in the pool. I suppose it is your pool." Anda could not quite believe the words coming from her mouth. "Please forgive me. You are a horse. How is it that you can speak?"

CHILD OF DAWN

The horse pawed at the ground. "How is it that a human is of lesser intelligence than a beast?"

Anda blushed. "You are speaking to me, but how?"

The horse stepped closer. "I can see your mind. I see your thoughts. All the things spinning around like a broken clock, going nowhere."

Anda took a step back. "What are you?"

The horse stepped closer. "Hop onto my back and I will show you."

There was something so intoxicating about this creature. Its frame rippled with muscle under its shimmering black coat. Anda could not understand why she wanted so desperately to touch something she feared. An invisible power radiated like the sun reflecting off glass from the creature, pulling her towards it. She let her dress fall from her hand and took a step towards the horse. The horse nickered softly and lowered its head so that Anda could climb up on its back. Reaching out, she gripped a handful of mane in her hand, and with the other, she gently stroked the horse's neck and shoulders, and ran them down its back. Its coat felt like water between her fingers.

Anda pulled her hand away from its neck only to find it fastened by some unseen force. She could not pull her hand away, nor could she remove her other hand from the mane. She tried to pull way more forcefully but could not. As she tried to free herself, the horse's mane began to move as though it were caught in the wind. But as she watched, it shifted and changed into streaming rivulets of water. The horse flicked its tail and it too turned to water. The horse turned its head to look at her. Its eyes had turned from a muted amber to a raving green. They cut through Anda, turning her heart to ice.

"Foolish child," it hissed to her mind, "Now you are mine for your undoing."

The horse reared up on its hind legs, pulling Anda off the ground. She hung there, helpless, unable to scream. It plunged down to earth and turned its head toward the water. It pawed at the earth and then began to gallop toward the water. Anda realized in one sickening instant that the horse meant to drag her to a watery grave. She could not breathe. She tried to dig her heels into the earth, but the horse was too immense to be reckoned with. She gathered every bit of strength she had, threw her head back, and screamed.

Her scream brought a raging gust of wind and the skies blackened over the trees. She saw Vandre crash through the branches and his face turn an ashen white. He lunged for the horse's mane, only to be knocked to the ground. Anda turned her head and looked at him over her shoulder. He pushed himself up and screamed after them.

"Droime! No!"

The horse ignored him and sped faster toward the water. Anda closed her eyes. She felt them leave the ground as the horse leaped upward and outward over the water. She hung helpless, flapping about like a hapless rag doll.

And then, she was no longer moving. Indeed, it was as though time itself had stopped. The wind ceased to howl and crash against her face. Her captor ceased to move in mid-flight. Even the water was silenced. She dared to open her eyes and look about.

He was there.

He stood a few feet below her dangling feet. He looked up at her with the same intense gaze she had looked at her when she had first seen his face. She felt caught between the madness of the horse and the uneasiness his gaze brought. He lifted his hands and raised them toward her. The horse began to move gently downward. It whinnied in protest but made no attempt to escape. He pulled them towards the shore with some unforeseen force. Anda felt her feet sink into the earth once more and she gasped a sigh of relief.

He approached them and slowly raised his hand to the horse's watery mane. As he touched the watery tendrils, they once again changed into a silken mane. He pulled the horse's head to his face and firmly whispered in its ear, "Droime, release."

Anda felt the weight of the horse lifted from her body and she fell backward. He caught her in his arms, and she fell against his chest. She buried his face in the folds of his clothes, afraid to look at him, or the horse.

"She was trespassing, my lord," Anda once more heard the horse's voice in her head.

"And she will learn the rules of the forest in time, Droime. She is under my protection. You would do well to remember it."

"My Lord Dagsbrún, if we welcome all outsiders, our sanctum will soon become the antithesis of a sanctuary."

Dagsbrún lifted her up to stand beside him. "I care not for your philosophy. Try to harm her again, and your own murky depths will be your grave."

The horse tossed its head and snorted. It turned and galloped toward the water. Lifting its front hooves off the ground, it leaped into the air. As it did so, its body turned into a rippling mass of shimmering water. It turned its head, looked at Dagsbrún, and plunged into the water.

Anda pushed herself away from her would-be rescuer and he smiled at her indignation. "You are quite welcome. I should have thought that head of yours was wiser than to listen to an idea I am assuming came from Vandre."

Vandre limped to their side. "I had thought she would enjoy a bath."

"And you thought to let her bathe in Solv. Tell me, did you arrange it with Droime, or thought to simply impede on his serious lack of hospitality?"

Vandre grimaced. "The last we had heard he was stalking the Southlands. He must have just returned."

Dagsbrún nodded. "Two days ago. While you were in the woods scrounging up halflings to bring to the castle."

"Again, my lord, I did not think…"

"Perhaps you should stop thinking and make a bit more effort in regard to being obedient!" Dagsbrún's voice shook the trees.

Vandre's eyes fell and Anda could bear it no more. "How dare you! Vandre is the only one who has been the slightest bit decent to me! You call yourself a lord, but you have all the animals of an animal!"

Vandre pulled at her arm. "Anda, watch your words…"

She shrugged him off. "No! As your prisoner, I command you to either treat me as a guest or lock me in your dungeons! Do not dangle me between the two! Here," she held up her hands and crossed them at the wrist. "Bind me! Drag me away! But do not pretend to care when you do not have the capacity for it!"

Dagsbrún stifled. He clenched his fists and scowled at her. "Vandre, go home."

"My lord…"

"Do as I say!" He grabbed Anda's hand, pulling her deeper into the woods. "And do not dare to follow!"

Chapter 6

The woods pressed closed upon them as they plunged into the wood. The whiteness of the branches she had seen near the castle and pond grew to an ashen gray. Knotted roots mingled with fragmented branches and the whole place groaned under the weight of its age and memories.—Tiny purple, red, and white flowers grew in the folds of the tree trunks and along the ground between tiny toadstools.

Anda was certain she could hear the forest breathe. Slight, labored breathing, like someone waiting to pass from the world. The branches swayed with intake and outtake of its life. Leaves whose life had already ended broke from their home in the trees and clustered about her feet, every so often rising on a breeze to dance their ghostly dance around her. Dagsbrún pulled her relentlessly deeper and deeper into the wood. His grip was merciless and his pace unforgiving. She half ran, half slid behind him, wondering where they were going and if she would ever come out again.

They rounded a bend in the trees and Dagsbrún stopped so suddenly that Anda hit him squarely in the shoulders. Ahead of them in the clearing lay the old ruins of an ancient stone structure. The forest had long since reclaimed the space as its own, climbing in and out of the stones with branches and moss.

Dagsbrún turned his head to look at her, raising a slender finger to his lips.

"Quiet, the forest is listening."

Anda rubbed her shoulders. "Trees have ears?"

He nodded. "And eyes, and lips. If they know you are here, they will share the gossip with brothers beyond the Vale."

She let her hands fall to her side. "They can do that?"

He looked at her with amusement. "Of course, they can. They speak with the *vind tunge,* the wind tongue. It carries beyond this world. And if the trees beyond the Vale know the gossip, those that dwell here will learn of it soon enough."

Anda swallowed. "What is it like? Beyond the Vale?"

He turned towards her. "Did your elf mother tell you nothing?"

She lowered her eyes. "She died before I ever really knew her. My father was the one who told me stories of where she came from. But he himself read those stories from books." She glanced up at him and thought she saw a faint hint of sympathy in his eyes.

The woods let out an immeasurable groan and Dagsbrún looked away. He strode to one of the larger trees and put his ear against it. The tree moaned and sighed, bending in the breeze. Gently, he raised a hand to the trunk and whispered softly under his breath. Then he reached into his waistcoat and pulled out a slim, slender dagger.

"What are you doing?" Anda asked, her heart quickening its pace.

"The forest is dying; it needs to be nourished." Without explaining further, he deftly cut the palm of his hand and held it up to the tree.

Anda watched with wide eyes as the veins in Dagsbrún's forearm and hand turned a deep golden color. She could see the color course through his arm and hand into the tree. Slowly veins in his upper arm, neck, and face filled with this golden hue until he was illuminated from within. Whatever it was, spread outward into the tree, lighting its roots to the same golden shade. Once the entire tree was alight, he pulled his hand away. The light subsided, and he stepped backward, cradling his arm as he did so. Anda watched as the cut in his hands healed to nothing but a small, white scar before her eyes.

She could find no words. She stood completely dumbfounded. Who was this man, this *being* before her? How could one so callous show such tenderness? She swallowed and looked away, suddenly feeling as though she had been privy to something she should not have seen. As though the exchange between Dagsbrún and the tree should have been one of great privacy.

"Come now," she heard his voice beside her. "It is no shameful thing to aid another thing."

She looked up at him. "What *are* you?"

The corners of his mouth turned up ever so slightly. "What are *you*?" She looked at him with confusion, and he sighed. "You know nothing of who you are, do you?"

He once more took her hand and pulled her toward the stone runs. Old steps, now a pile of rubble, led to a stone foundation. In the middle was the remains of what she guessed to be a doorway. Two pillars stood about 6 feet tall with an archway overhead that remained whole, despite being covered in ivy and dirt.

He let her hand fall and approached the archway. Once more he took out the knife and held it over his hand. He looked over his shoulder at her and then cut swiftly and deep. Raising his palm, slammed it into the rocks of one of the pillars. Instantly, they exploded with the same golden hue that had ignited the tree. But this time, Dagsbrún's body did not light up as it had done before, instead, the pillars seemed to draw life from his body. He arched his back and his face contorted in pain, but he did not move his hand.

The ground trembled and the forest seethed. Anda ran up the remaining steps and threw herself at him. "Stop it! You will kill us!"

He did not look at her but stared at the space between the pillars. "Watch!" He yelled.

She turned her head and stared at the seemingly empty space. Slowly, that space began to move and alter, as though she were watching a mirage in the desert. The forest disappeared, and she beheld a vast wasteland of rocky terrain laced with deep canyons. Her knees gave way and she fell against the pillar.

Dagsbrún grimaced, convulsing as though he was being struck by some invisible force. The image before them shifted to a vast field, laden with soldiers. They were piled upon one another, two deep in some places. They crawled upon one another, as countless as grains of sand. Metal rang against metal and Anda covered her ears.

As she watched the battle before her, she came to realize that those who fought were elves, and she wondered why they fought one another. She could make no differentiation between the sides. Both wore the same armor, their hair in long, flaxen locks, with their ears protruding proudly from beneath their helmets. She heard a screech and turned her focus to the horizon beyond the pillars. Black beasts appeared against the clouds, seemingly flying toward both her and the elvish battle. As the shapes grew closer, she saw that they were not beasts, but men. Tall men with great wings that spread twice the height of their bodies. They wore robes of black and had skin as pale as the full moon. These men dove into the throng of elves. They picked the elves up one by one by their hair and flew several feet off the ground. Hovering there, these creatures revealed long, fanged teeth that flashed white and sharp. Forcing the flailing elves' heads to one side, they sank these teeth into their necks and drank the blood of their victims. Once their prey ceased to move, they dropped them back to the ground, to be trampled by the turmoil below.

Anda screamed.

Dagsbrún ripped his hand from the pillar, and the battle vanished. He fell backward to the ground, heaving and gasping for air. He groaned and spread himself prostrate on the ground.

Anda lowered her arms, tears cascading down her face. She looked at the pillars and archway, now void and silent, then at Dagsbrún. He had ceased to move, and she wondered if his conjuring had been beyond the powers he possessed.

But then, he gasped and rolled himself to his side. Color began to return to his face, and he looked up at her with what she thought to be immense sadness in his eyes. "It has grown worse. The darkness is spreading."

Anda shuddered. "What was that? Where, and *when* was that?"

He coughed and sat up. "That, dear, naive, halfling was what the world is like beyond the Vale. The world that rules our blood." He looked at her. "Well, at least half of yours."

She stood and crossed to the archway, placing her hands on its cold surface. "But…"

He stood to his feet. "It is a doorway to that world." He leaned against the archway. "Many years ago, the elves would travel between worlds, caring for the forests and the fields. They were the shepherds of the earth, and all within their care flourished."

"And then?"

He sank once more to the ground. "And then, Man set himself up as superior in all things. He drove the elf back, destroying all the doors they could find. This is the last one that I know of."

"But what did I see? Why were the elves fighting one another? And those men with wings… what were they?"

Dagsbrún coughed again. "So many questions. That is what that world has become. Brother fighting brother, enemies who were once kingdoms living side by side. And all the anger and hatred from simply being different." He sighed, and it seemed to Anda as though a great sadness had settled on him. He used the support of the pillar to pull himself to his feet once more. "But I am not gifted with recitations. That is Gammel's gift. Come." He offered her his hand. "The day grows long, and I have wasted the morning chasing after you."

She took his hand and followed him down the steps. "But why show me? Why bring me here to this place that wreaks of death and is filled with all sorts of nightmares and monsters?"

He stiffened and slowed his pace. "Sometimes the monster is not who or what you think it is."

"I fail to see how I could be mistaken. A horse that would enchant me, only to drown me. Visions of elves killing elves in a haunted forest where the trees themselves act as spies! Tell me, how could I misunderstand any of this?"

"There are two sides to every reflection!" He snapped. "You look in the mirror and you think you see what you are supposed to see." He gripped her shoulders. "But what if... what if you only saw what you convinced yourself you *should* see? And what if your reflection, what was actually there, was something entirely different?"

She quivered under his grip. His cold fingers sent pangs of fear to her heart. She met his iron gaze with her own. "And what does your reflection tell you? Are you a man or a monster?"

He let go of her shoulders and stumbled backward, visibly stung by her words. "I am no man," he growled, as though the very word sickened him to say. "And you would do well to remember it." With that, he turned on his heel and disappeared into the shadows.

Anda regretted her harsh words. Perhaps he had not intended to terrify her so. True, he was her captor. But she was slowly coming to the realization that there was a part of him that perhaps lay hidden. Perhaps, she did not know as much as she thought she did. And perhaps, just perhaps she was wrong about Lord Dagsbrún.

Chapter 7

They walked back to the castle in silence. Once inside its walls, Dagsbrún had vanished from sight, leaving Anda standing alone at the foot of a great staircase. Gammel and Vandre were nowhere to be found and therefore she found the castle to be full of nothing but silence. Feeling as though she was quite alone, she decided to explore her expansive prison.

To her left and her right were a series of rooms. Most were shut off from sight, save one. She crossed the floor to peek into what appeared to be a study. The air was saturated with the smell of leather bindings and old pages. Anda pushed the door open and stepped inside. The room was dimly lit with several worn-down candles. The floorboards creaked under her feet, and she paused to listen. The castle maintained its silence. She crossed the floor to a small table and picked up a candle. Lifting it toward the ceiling she gasped softly.

Books. Books everywhere. Books lined shelves that disappeared up into the shadows. They were a rainbow of monochromatic colors—navy, burgundy, black, and gold. Their covers were worn, and some had their pages lying naked on the shelf. Some shelves had pages stacked haphazardly with no bindings at all. She reached out and gently pulled a small book from the shelf. Holding to her nose, she inhaled the sweet mustiness of its age and use. It smelt of mystery and memory.

She gently opened the cover and read the first page. *The Saga of Morginn and Avundil.* Anda sighed. Poetry. How she missed reading her mother's books beside a warm fire. She gently placed the book back on the shelf and turned to leave the room. Perhaps Dagsbrún would let her read some of his books.

Perhaps they could read them together…

Anda slammed the door shut, causing an echo to bounce down the long corridor. What was she thinking? Where had that thought come from? Why would she want to read with *him*, her captor? She shook such an absurd thought out of her head and continued her exploration. The castle was immense and seemingly empty of any life. She thought for a moment of escape but then shook that idea from her head as well. She knew if she tried, some beast or Dagsbrún himself would materialize out of the shadows and drag her back. She walked through room after room. Some were full of ornate chairs and tables; others were completely barren. There was a complete juxtaposition between rooms that suggested wealth and royalty and those that implied total poverty.

There was no sign of life. Anywhere. No sign that anyone had once dwelt within the walls of the castle. But things were clean, and so Anda wondered if Vandre was tasked with keeping things tidy. Though she could not see him doing it all on his own. She moved through what appeared to be a dining room, through a narrow corridor, and into the storerooms and kitchen. Metal pots hung above a large wooden table, swaying in some invisible breeze. The shelves were bare, save for a few cobwebs. She searched the storeroom's food and found little. What did they eat? And where did it come from?

Moving through another door, she came back out to the great hall at the foot of the stairs. She gripped the banister and slowly made her way up the great staircase. It seemed to climb higher than she remembered the castle to be. Higher and higher she climbed, passing floor after floor until she reached the top. The stairs opened to a yawning corridor. The walls were lined with faded tapestries, some hanging by only a few threads. This floor had no windows or doors, save at the very end. There stood an immense wooden door, carved with garish faces; all with mouths opened in either screams or yawns.

Anda crept toward the door. Something about this floor felt different. Not only did it feel as though there was an absence of life, but it felt as though there was also an absence of air. She felt as though she were moving toward some unseen vortex, being drawn into nothingness. There was an aroma of age and decay, as though memory itself had died in the hallways. She rested her hand on the rough surface of the door and traced the mouth of one of the figures, wondering what horrors they had suffered to scream so. Then, summoning all her courage in one breath, she pushed the door open. It groaned and heaved as though it had not been touched in centuries. As the door separated itself from its frame a gust of musty air streamed out from behind it. Anda coughed and sputtered and then peered into the room.

It was drenched in silence. The walls and floors were barren except for a thick layer of dust and several garlands of finely spun cobwebs. She pushed the door open further and crept inside. Her feet left prints along the dusty floor and the motion of her body made the cobwebs sway. On the far end of the room, there was a window. It was void of any trappings or shutters and took up a majority of the wall. Crossing the floor, she placed her hands on the sill and peered out.

Before her eyes lay a patchwork view of the entire land. Directly below were the trees of the forest. They seemed to stretch for miles to the east and west. To the north, beyond the forest, she could glimpse the pastureland and the horizon, shielded on both sides by the mountains, capped in their snowy adornments.

She sighed and leaned against the wall. How close and contracting had felt just a short time ago. Now, it was only a small speck in a world she never knew even existed. Her mind wandered to what her father and sister were doing at that moment. Were the sheep in the pasture or the barn? Had the mists left with her? Was her family finally free of the town's condemnation? Would they no longer be plagued now that she was gone?

Gone.

The word pricked her heart. To her, it seemed an incredibly definite term, as though it sealed her in her fate. Her absence was their salvation, but it was also her heartbreak. And now, now was trapped in this place of immensity and mystery—a place filled with a magic she could not understand.

Suddenly, the hair on the back of her neck stood on end. Her skin grew cold, and she had the intense feeling that she was being watched. She spun around, thinking to see someone there, but the room was empty. Her senses heightened and she felt as though she could hear the cobwebs wisp across the ceiling. She glanced up at the rafters and narrowed her eyes. The shadows seemed to shift with the movement of the sun, playing tricks on her eyes. The dark corners shifted with the grayness of the beams and stretched out into a pale brown.

And then... then the shadows pulled away from the rafters and moved down the walls. They twisted and cascaded into the shapes of humans. They crawled across the floor towards her and shifted even more into the shape of women.

Anda shrank against the wall, wishing she could grow wings and fly from the room. The women floated from crawling on all fours to an upright position. There were three of them, all similarly in height and build. Their skin was so pale, it was almost translucent. Pale blue and green veins could be seen under the surface of their skin, but they did not pulse with the beat of a heart. Despite their pallor, Anda was breathless at the sight of their beauty. Their eyes were the color of jade, and their faces were etched like a marble statue. Long, dark hair cascaded down their backs to the floor, brushing against the bare soles of their feet. They were clothed in a fabric that floated about their legs, and yet hugged the curve of their hips and torsos. It was a grayish hue and rustled almost melodically as they crossed the floor.

They paused a few feet from Anda, staring at her with their piercing eyes. The tallest of the three tilted her head to the side and smiled. Anda could see her teeth flash, even in the shadows. She reached out her hand toward Anda, her fingers clawing at the light.

"Why do you disturb our sleep, halfling?" Her voice was melodic, mesmerizing, almost more like a musical instrument than a voice.

Anda swallowed. "I did not know that anyone lived here besides Dagsbrún and his servants."

The second one laughed a shrill, bitter laugh. "Do you see? He keeps us a secret!"

"Hush," hissed the third. "He does not keep us a secret. He has quite forgotten about us."

Anda managed a smile. "I do not think anyone could forget ladies such as yourself." She managed a small curtsy. "My name is Anda."

"Sweet child," the first one smiled at her. "I am Morsdog. The one with the voice like an eagle's shriek is Gudinne and the old one is Sybil."

"Old!" The one called Sybil hissed. "You are far older than me!"

"And I am far younger than you both!" cackled Gudinne. She ran her fingers through her hair. "And far more beautiful than you ever were in life."

"Hush, you fool!" Morsdog slapped Gudinne across the face.

Anda cringed. "Were in life? I do not understand."

"We are the Vondod," Sybil replied. "The undead."

Anda felt the room spin. "The undead? But how?"

Morsdog's countenance changed from one of indifference to one of leering menace. "We are Dagsbrún's playthings. His conquests. He has kept us locked in the wing of his castle for his entertainment. Keeping us alive on scraps. But now you are here, and all of that will change."

Anda swallowed. "How does my presence make it change?"

Gudinne snickered. "Because you… are fresh meat."

Morsdog raised her arms over her head and the wind howled swept into the room. The sky darkened, lengthening the shadows in the room, and diminishing the light. As the shadows crept toward Anda, so did the three beings. She realized that their pale skin must be incapable of exposure to sunlight.

"Come here, child," Sybil hissed. "Don't make us chase you."

"I want the first bite," Gudinne moaned.

Anda pressed her body against the wall and Morsdog chuckled. "That right belongs to me." In one blurred motion, her hand was around Anda's neck, pushing her against the wall. She tilted her head back and opened her mouth. Long, slender white teeth protruded from her pink gums.

Anda screamed, but her cries were muffled by the hand squeezing the life from her. "Please," she whispered. "Please."

"Not too tight, dearie," Sybil hissed. "You will turn her blood cold."

Morsdog leered. "It will not have time to turn cold." She bent Anda's neck to the side and moved closer. "So sweet, so refreshing," she breathed into Anda's ear.

"Hurry up! Hurry up!" Gudinne laughed. "We are hungry!"

Suddenly, there was a rush of wind and light tumbled into the room. The wraiths screamed in pain and flew back into the shadowed corners. Anda fell to the floor, gasping for air.

CHILD OF DAWN

Blackness crept across her vision as she fought to stay conscious. She felt as though she were falling, hurdling toward some distant ground, but never finding it.

She felt a presence beside her and forced her eyes to open. There, kneeling over her, was Dagsbrún. His eyes glowed with an iridescent blue hue, much brighter than she remembered them being. His arms were stretched over her as though to protect her and his lips were turned up in an animalistic snarl.

"You dare to touch something that belongs to me?" His voice was so low that the ground rumbled with its intensity.

"We belong to you!" Morsdog screamed.

"And you ignore us!" Gudinne wrung her hands. "We are yours, and you toss us aside like old playthings!"

"You are old playthings!" he snarled. "But that is your doing, and the doing of the Vale!"

"Politics aside, my lord, we must eat. We are hungry." Sybil's voice sounds like rusted hinges.

"Have some manners, then," Dagsbrún grumbled. "You weren't always beasts. Go to the kitchen and Vandre will feed you."

"Scraps!" Gudinne shrieked. "Scraps for ladies! What have we become?"

"Control yourself!" Morsdog slapped Gudinne. "We must maintain some sort of dignity."

Dagsbrún snickered. "You lost that when you crossed over." He picked Anda up in his arms. "Now go. Vandre is waiting for you."

"What is to become of the halfling?" Sybil whimpered.

Gudinne cackled. "She will fade away, just like us!"

"Indeed," Morsdog growled. "He will ruin her. Just wait and see!"

"Be gone!" Dagsbrún leapt to his feet. The three wraiths crawled along the wall and up into the rafters, clinging to the stone and wooden beams like reptilian creatures. He watched them creep back into the shadows until they disappeared into the darkness. Then scooped up Anda in his arms and dashed for the door.

In her semi-conscious state, Anda was aware of two things. The first was being incredibly certain that Dagsbrún had not paused to open the door. Therefore, she concluded that he had either left the door open—though she did not remember him opening the door, nor did she recall him coming through it- or that he possessed some sort of power by which to open doors without touching them.

She thought that it was quite preposterous that she favored the second notion more than the first.

The second thing she was aware of was how Dagsbrún smelled. Scents of leather and honey wafted from the folds of his clothes, sweetness mixed with age. He smelt of memory and magic. She turned her head toward his chest and rested it there. The fragrance of honey changed to that of oranges ripe in the Autumn and she got a whiff of cloves and nutmeg. It was intoxicating.

He carried her down flight after flight of stairs until at last she heard him kick open a door with his foot. *Perhaps this door was not susceptible to his magic,* she thought.

She opened her eyes just enough to see that they were in Gammel's workroom once more. A fire roared in the fireplace, and she could see the wizened old elf sitting in a high-back chair gazing intently into the flames.

"Gammel!" Dagsbrún shouted. "Help me with her!"

Gammel did not move his gaze from the fire. "So many questions swirling in the light," he muttered. "So many riddles left unanswered."

Dagsbrún stiffened. "No riddles now, old man! She needs your help!"

Gammel sighed. "No, Dagsbrún. You need her help. *We* need her help. There is a difference."

"The Vondod nearly made a feast out of her," Dagsbrún gently placed her in the chair opposite Gammel. "Morsdog would have sucked the life from her, had I not come."

Gammel reached across and gently grasped Anda's wrist. "She is unharmed, save perhaps her nerves." He let her wrist fall and rose from his chair. Crossing to the table strewn with parchment, he gently picked on up to examine it. "Tell me, Dagsbrún. How did you know the halfling was in peril?"

Dagsbrún blinked. "What do you mean?"

Gammel sighed. "How did you know Anda was being threatened by those Harpies?"

Dagsbrún shrugged. "I am not sure. I just knew."

"Nonsense, boy!" Gammel tossed the parchment aside and turned to Dagsbrún. "There is no just knowing!" He gripped Dagsbrún's shoulders. "Tell me, did you hear her scream? Did you see the Vondod enter the room where she was?"

"Of course not. You know as well as I do that the tower room bears no entrance beside the one door and window."

"A door that is covered in enchantment and still the halfling managed to open it."

Dagsbrún cast his gaze on the young woman in the chair. "I know. I thought of that," he replied softly.

"So then answer me, how did you know she needed help?"

Dagsbrún shrugged. "I do not know. I suppose it was a feeling."

Gammel's eyes brightened. "A feeling? What kind of feeling?"

Dagsbrún closed his eyes. "It was as though she were beside me. Standing there, telling me she was in danger. She spoke to me as though were speaking to one another in front of the fire."

"She spoke to you?"

Dagsbrún's brow furrowed. "Yes. I mean, it felt that way. But she was on the opposite side of the castle. So how could that be?"

Gammel's mouth turned up at the corners. "Because you two have the *Forbindelse.*"

"Forbindelse?"

Gammel nodded. "A connection that transcends."

Dagsbrún burst into laughter. "Your herbs are making you lose your wit, old man."

Gammel picked up the parchment once more. "It is written in the old texts. Our world was founded on our ancestor's ability to communicate, to connect, through feeling one another's feelings and emotions."

"Those are bedtime stories!" Dagsbrún scoffed.

Gammel's voice softened. "Your parents had it."

Dagsbrún crossed to where Gammel had been sitting and threw himself into the chair. He clasped his fingers together and rested his chin on them. "You know what I am, Gammel. You know ALL that I am. How could you even consider such a thing? Never mind the fact that I am her captor, there is nothing between us." He threw his arms up in the air. "How could there be? I do not have a heart, nor even a soul. How I could I even hope to be anything but a monster to her?"

Gammel leaned against the table. "She is no mere human, only half. She possesses her mother's goodness."

Dagsbrún looked up at him. "You knew her mother?"

"Not well, but I knew of her. Though the halfling does not know that." He smiled. "You are more alike than you would care to admit."

"How so?"

"You both have spirit. And both of you are afraid of what you could be if only you believed in yourself. But you are afraid to embrace the reflection you see in the mirror."

Dagsbrún jumped to his feet. "I am not afraid!" he roared. "I have nothing to fear! What in this world or the other could harm me?"

"Indeed, what killed your parents?"

Anda groaned in her chair and Dagsbrún turned to look at her. The air seemed to constrict in his chest. "I can't. I won't," he whispered. Pulling his cloak about him, he turned and ran out of the room.

Chapter 8

Anda groaned again and opened her eyes. The warmth from the fire made her feel drowsy. She rolled her head to look at Gammel. "What happened?"

Gammel smiled. "Clever minx. You know as well as I do you were awake the whole time."

Anda pushed herself to a sitting position. "How do you know that?

The elf laughed. "Your heartbeat. Had you been truly unconscious, it would have slowed. But instead, it beat faster as our conversation progressed."

Anda glared at him. "You are a devil."

"I am an elf and a wizard. There is not much that I do not see."

"If you know everything, then why did you not stop those monsters?"

Gammel laughed once more. "Just because I possess knowledge, does not mean I can interrupt the course of your life."

Anda's eyes narrowed. "I have always heard that the elvish race was one of protectors."

Gammel eased himself into his chair. "We are protectors of what is good, yes. But we are also teachers. You must learn to find your own goodness."

Anda sighed. "You speak in riddles."

"I speak what I know."

"If you are so wise, then tell me... what is this connection you speak of? This *Forbindelse?*" Anda's voice softened. "And is it true? Did you know my mother?"

Gammel leaned forward. "Shall I tell you a fairy tale story, halfling? And shall you then tell me what you think of it?"

"I feel as though I will listen and know less than I already do. But as I am a prisoner in this place, what else am I to do?

He threw a log into the fire and sat back. "You are far more than a prisoner. Far more than you know. Now, watch." He took his hand and whispered something into it. A tiny beam of light sprang up and spread across his hand. Muttering a second incantation, he tossed the beam of light into the fire, and the room was flooded with a burst of bluish-green light. A gray mist poured over the table and from it the tall figure of an elf arose.

"What is this?" Anda gasped.

"A history lesson," Gammel responded. He moved his hand and the figure turned and looked directly at Anda. "Centuries ago, when our race was new and young, the great elfish leader, Skaperen, saw it in his wisdom to bind our race to certain laws so that we would not fall into dissent as so many other races had. He used a deep magic that could not be altered nor changed. All these laws were bound to one book—The *Regelen*.

Anda raised an eyebrow. "The elves do not seem like a race that bends to the will of an ancient elf, or outdated book."

Gammel nodded. "For a time, we did. For a time, there was harmony, and we went about our tranquil lives, keeping to ourselves, and enjoying our peace. But then, one of us decided that it was not enough to just *be*, we needed to *live.*"

"So, someone became a miscreant?"

"The law was specific. We were not to associate with other races. Human or vampire. Humans were relatively easy to stay away from, we simply did not cross the Vale. Vampires were a different matter. For those of us who were younger, their species was a tantalizing fruit dangling in front of us. The *Regelen* could tell us what not to do, but it could not suppress our natural instincts, nor our insatiable curiosity. The vampires were experts in luring their prey and they were beautiful to behold."

"When they are not busy destroying you," Anda quipped.

"Ljosalfar was the fairest of the elves. She radiated light. She was all that was good and kind in our world. And then, she wandered beyond our borders and met Raefn."

"Raefn?"

"A vampire. He was truly something to behold. Immense and powerful. Seductive. He felt the same way about his existence as Ljosalfar did. Together, they began to push the boundaries of their laws. With Ljosalfar, Raefn learned he could control his thirst. With him, she learned that her elfish magic was somehow amplified. They fell uncontrollably in love. It was the first time the *forbindelse* existed outside our race. They were bonded, and there was nothing to be done about it."

"But something *was* done about it?"

Gammel nodded. "They ran away and hand-fasted in secret. The elders from both the elves and the vampires hunted them like animals and finally found them." A shadow crossed over Gammel's face. "Ljosalfar had given birth to a child, a perfect mix of both elvish and vampire blood."

"What happened?"

"They killed both. An elder drove a stake through Ljosalfar into Raefn. She died in his arms shortly before he burned alive from the inside out."

Anda bit her lip. "And the baby?"

Gammel leaned heavily on his staff. "Ljosalfar gave the baby to an elf named Drotin. He took the infant and fled the Vale, changing his name and hiding the baby in an obscure castle in a wood."

Anda's eyes widened. "You!"

He nodded. "I was once second only to Skaperen. He was my grandfather. When my father was killed, Skaperen took me in and raised me. I idolized him. But he became obsessed with power, and his laws made the elves arrogant. Ljosalfar was everything to me and he took her with the desire to control. And so, I was Drotin no more. I became Gammel."

"She was your daughter?"

"Granddaughter. Making her child my great-grandson. I took the infant and hid him far beyond the Vale, hoping he would never be found. Hoping elves and vampires alike would stay in their world and leave this one to us."

Anda felt her heart leap into her throat. "Dagsbrún is…"

New lines seemed to form on Gammel's face as he spoke. "He is my own flesh and bone." He stood and crossed to the doorway. "At least in part."

"But he treats you like a common servant!"

Gammel smiled. "Dagsbrún is a wild and relentless thing. His nature is to dominate everything around him. It always has been. I am content to serve him in doing all I can to keep him safe until the time when he can take his rightful place?"

"Has he not already taken more than what is rightfully his?"

Gammel turned to look at her. "His life is not one of ease, halfling. He might have convinced you otherwise with the I he wears daily. But he is tormented."

Anda looked back at the fire. "Tormented? By his guilt? His need to kidnap innocent women?"

"I believe found you and brought you here willingly."

"And what of the monsters upstairs?" Anda gripped the arms of the chair. "Did they come willingly? Or did he seduce them into the state they are now in?"

Gammel sighed. "Quite the opposite." He turned and crossed back to the table. "While we are powerful beings, there is a limit to that power. And those who are foolish enough to think anyone can control that power usually suffer for it."

"You blame those poor... things for their condition?"

"When Skaperen created The *Regelen*, he tied all elves to its magic. That meant that any elf, living at the time, or existing in the distant future had to abide by its rules. The law says that we can only exist in our lands. If we leave, our powers will wane, and destruction will befall us. When Morsdog, Gudinne, and Sybil heard the rumor of an elf living beyond the Vale, they broke the law and came to your world in pursuit of him. He was a youth at the time, far younger and more foolish than he is now. At first, he relished the attention, not having any company besides myself—Vandre did not come to us until much later. Despite the attention, Dagsbrún soon realized that he preferred to be on his own, as he had been his entire life. But three of them would not leave."

"Why not?"

"Dagsbrún was irresistible to them. He was alluring and enticing, without particularly trying. His father's race had that power."

"To seduce?"

Gammel shook his head. "It wasn't seduction. It was magnetic. They thought of him as some sort of powerful thing that they could boast about interacting with. It drove them quite mad."

"So, he did not try and make them leave?"

"No, he did. In fact, after a while, he begged them to. Once they were gone from their homes, their bodies began to change. Their skin began to separate from their bones, they did not wish to eat, and the light dimmed in their eyes. And still, they would not leave."

"What did he do?"

"The asking turned to begging. But he also knew that if they were to return to the Vale, they would either die in trying or be killed the moment they entered Elfish lands. And yet if they stayed here, and he did not intervene, they would continue to suffer."

"Anda began to feel faint once more. "And so, he intervened?"

Gammel sighed. "Dagsbrún told them that what he could offer was not death, but also not life. But their pain would be gone. They were conniving wretches and knew that if he did what he was offering, they would be forever connected to him. In their maddened state, they believed that this connection would be a *forbindelse*."

"They were mistaken?"

"Horrifically so. Dagsbrún grudgingly agreed to turn them into what he, and they thought he was. But it did not cure them. Instead, it only accentuated all that was not good in them. At first, they were ravenous hunters, stalking the woods and feeding on anything that moved. As they aged, they became frail and even more pitiful. Their obsession with Dagsbrún turned into bitterness. And he, regretting all his interactions with them, felt compelled to care for them until whatever fate ultimately befell them. And so, they haunt the tower, hunting and feeding themselves when they can. And when they cannot, Dagsbrún sees to it that they have some form of nourishment."

Anda stared silently for a moment into the flames and then turned and looked at Gammel. "Will that fate befall me?"

Gammel chuckled. "You are not some flighty elf, Anda."

"No, I am a halfling with no one searching for me and nowhere to go. If I were to remain a prisoner here, I would do so with no one knowing or caring, except perhaps my father. And he has resigned himself to not come for me."

Gammel went to a shelf lined with books and pulled one covered in dust from the assortment. He set it on the table and unclasped a metal lock etched in gold. He thumbed through the pages until he found the page he was looking for. He ran his fingers over the words, letting them rest halfway down the page. "I believe, Anda, that you are not here by chance."

She chuckled. "Yes, I am sure it was predestined that I become the bane of my village, flee for my life, and end up here."

"There is a prophecy..."

Anda held up her hand. "Wait. I do not wish to hear something with which you will try and convince me that I am part of some manifested plan."

"Just let me read it, will?" Gammel ran his fingers once more over the text as though to be certain he was reading the correct thing, and then spoke with resolve:

When one that is half, meets one that is two halves of a whole, then shall there be peace among chaos, unity, and the rightful heir shall control.

For in their meeting, two worlds shall collide, and in their union, their kind shall abide.

The room was silent. Somewhere in a dark corner, water dripped from the rafters. Anda was very aware of the rhythm and beat with which it fell, like a slow hammer on a nail hammering into the finality of her existence. Slowly she stood and crossed to the table. She reached across and gently placed her hand over Gammel's. "I know this is what you want. I cannot imagine living through so many lifetimes and seeing so much destruction." She squeezed his hand tightly. "But I am not who you think I am. I do not have a *forbindelse* with Dagsbrún, or anyone else. I do not even know who I am. I am barely connected to myself."

Gammel's pulled his hand away, and he gripped his staff tightly. "Tell me, halfling. Why do you think you are still alive? Dagsbrún is half-elf, but he is also half-vampire. And that half is fueled by a lust for blood. A *need* for it. And yet, he has not raised a finger to you. In fact, he saved you from the kelpie. He saved you from the Vondod. How could you possibly not see that there is a reason he has let you live?"

"But I barely know him!"

"And he barely knows you. But the elf in you, your mother's blood, keeps him at bay. He recognizes a part of himself in you. Even if he does not know it."

"And what of my mother?" Anda could feel her blood begin to heat. "You said you knew of her? What, exactly, did you know?"

Gammel gave a half smile. "While Morsdog, Gudinne, and Sybil came to pursue the power that Dagsbrún had, your mother came for love. Much like Ljosalfar and Raefn, her love for your father was also absolutely forbidden. But their love was true, and he loved her for her spirit, not her magic. They gleaned what was good for one another, in the same way that Ljosalfar did for Raefn."

Anda was silent for a moment. "And you think it is I, an outcast, who will do that for Dagsbrún?"

Gammel nodded. "And he for you."

She laughed. "What could he possibly do for me?"

"Show you that you possess a power that, on your own, could create stars. But together, the two of you could create galaxies."

Anda scratched at the table's surface with her fingernail. "I have no power, except to anger others."

"It angers them because they do not understand. And it angers you because you do not know what you truly possess." Gammel gently took her hand and pulled her to the middle of the table. Reaching underneath, he produced a large silver bowl and placed it on the table. He lifted his staff and gently touched the middle of the bowl with it. A small silvery stream appeared at its tip and trickled into the bowl. "Watch," he whispered. "And learn." He touched the water with the tip of his finger and a glittery firmament swirled up out of the water. It stretched out over the surface of the table, sparkling in the candlelight. He looked at Anda and smiled. "Stars." He removed his finger from the water and leaned on his staff. "Now, you try."

Anda laughed. "You cannot be serious."

"I am most serious."

She looked at him with complete exasperation, but somehow knew he would not stop until she did as he asked. Sighing, she stepped toward the bowl, reached out her finger, and plunged it into the water.

"Gently," Gammel gently gripped her wrist. "Touch the water, do not attack it. Believe that you have the power. Feel it in your blood, in your heart."

Anda pulled her finger out. She closed her eyes and inhaled deeply. Opening her eyes, she fixed her eyes on the water. The rest of the room seemed to grow blurry, as though a light morning fog had crept in. The only thing clear in her vision was the bowl. It rippled, but there was no apparent source to the ripple. She raised her finger and gently placed the tip in the water. The ripples increased, and tiny waves cascaded over the rim of the bowl.

"Believe," Gammel whispered.

Anda once more closed her eyes and searched herself for this power the elf said she possessed. She sank into a blanket of darkness, climbing down into herself to find the tiniest of sparks. She searched her mind, her soul, and her heart—and she found it, hidden in a forgotten corner. With her thoughts, she reached out and seized it.

"Anda, open your eyes."

Anda peeked through one eyelid at the water. It had turned from a placid surface to a frothy firmament fixed with a vast expanse of stars. These sprang from the water like a geyser, up and out of the bowl and into the air. They swirled around Anda and Gammel in a flurry of light. Gammel gently took Anda's hand and raised it up into the sparkling current. The lights rose and fell over her fingers.

"How is it even possible?" she whispered.

"It came from within," Gammel's voice was filled with awe, as though he himself was surprised at what she had done.

"But, how?"

"You believed in yourself." He gripped her hand and lifted it towards the ceiling. The stars rose from the water and spread themselves across the roof. They grew brighter, their rays touching one another until the room was overwhelmed with light. And then, just as they had shown brightly, they dissipated into nothing, and the room was dark once more.

Anda felt a surge of energy leave her, and her legs gave way. She fell against Gammel, and he gently led her to sit in front of the fire. Darkness swam around the corners of her eyes and felt her body give way to unconsciousness. "Is it always so exhausting?" she gasped.

Gammel chuckled. "You will learn. That was quite impressive for your first time."

"I do not think that *was* my first time," she whispered. Gammel looked at her questioningly. "I think... I think I have used magic before. I just did not know I was."

Gammel studied her face. "How do you know?"

Her brow furrowed. "The villagers, they despised me. They said I was cursed. They called me a witch. I always hated them for calling me that. And yet, perhaps they were right. Their words angered me, and I think I returned their hatred by punishing them with the elements. When I fled, there was a storm, and even though I feared it... Perhaps I was the one who caused it. Even now, I feel the winds rage within me." She gripped her chest. "I thought it was fear, but now... now I feel as though it is an immense anger."

Gammel sat down across from her. "You should be angry. But let that anger give way to purpose. For while anger will drive you, a purpose will fulfill you."

Anda bit her lip. "But what is that purpose? Surely it cannot be to fall in love with someone who is holding me prisoner, someone whom I do not even know."

Gammel searched for an answer. She was not wrong in what she said, and yet, he believed that there was more to Anda's and Dagsbrún's stories. He rose and crossed the room to the doorway into the courtyard. Dark clouds were gathering overhead, and the air was heavy with moisture. He closed his eyes and muttered softly under his breath. Opening his eyes once more, looked toward the skies as the rain began to fall.

"Come here, halfling." Anda rose and crossed the room to stand beside him. Gently he took her hand once more and held it out in the rain. Droplets of water fell onto her fingers and cascaded into a tiny pool in her palm. "The rain is a part of the sky. It gathers and grows in the heavens, filling the clouds with water. And yet..." he pulled her down to kneel on the ground and placed her fingertip in a growing puddle. "When the earth needs it, the rain falls. It comes from its home to nourish the ground, to keep the meadows green, and the flowers tall. The rain and the earth are the most unlikely pair. In a world with no challenges, and no need for companionship, they would never meet. But the earth needs the rain, Anda. Much like Dagsbrún needs you."

Anda felt a tightening in her throat. "And what does the rain get from the earth? Nothing!"

Gammel shook his head. "On the contrary. The rain is given all the glory for the beauty the earth displays. All that is good in the earth comes from the rain. And the earth displays the rain's work with adoration." He let go of Anda's hand. "I do not pretend to think that what I ask of you is easy. But there is so much more to Dagsbrún, than what he allows you to see. I ask you to look at him with the eyes your mother gave you—past what is on the surface. Search out his heart. For while it is lost, you may find that it holds immense beauty if it is found."

She rose to her feet and wiped her face. "This is all too much."

Gammel raised a hand to comfort her, but she backed away. "Anda, I do not mean to frighten you, I only mean to help you."

"You mean to help him!" Tears welled up in her eyes. "I am a pawn in your chess game!"

"You are not a pawn; you are a queen. You matter much more than even Dagsbrún." He pushed himself up with his staff.

"But I do not wish it!" she screamed. Turning from him, she fled the room and all the revelations it held.

Chapter 9

Dagsbrún had left Gammel and Anda and roamed the empty halls of the castle for what seemed like hours. He felt caged, trapped... yet he did not understand why. He was not held here against his will; he was free to come and go as he pleased. He could stalk the forests or lay waste to a village. He was lord of a castle, the son of a prince.

The son of a traitor.

His birthright plagued him. It haunted him like the ghosts of those who had fallen prey to his bite. A war raged within him. A war between his mother's light, and his father's darkness. In truth, he wished he could follow them into the obliteration that had consumed them. But he could not. His fate was to live. A century after long century... wars, plagues, politics, and pestilence could not end his suffering.

His loneliness.

For that was the culmination of his misery. He could love for hatred of what had been done to his parents, to him. He could not possess empathy for his victims, for in their eyes he saw only those who hunted him with pitchforks and swords. And yet, when the night stretched out, and he lurked amongst its shadows, his soul would awaken to torment him with the reminder that there was none who could be his equal, none that could survive his touch or embrace. None that he could love, caress, or kiss without leading them to their death.

He had thought there had been a chance with the Vondod. Indeed, he remembered how he had felt a warmth creep into his heart when they had passed through the Vale and into his life. They had been so attentive, filling his days with what he had thought was affection and compassion.

But as the days turned to decades, he began to understand that their motives were far from noble. They squabbled like starving hens over whom he paid attention to, whom he cared for more. Morsdog searched him out in the night and begged to be turned. Sybil found him in the hallways and asked him to preserve her youth. And Gudinne, Gudinne would lurk in the corners and wail how she was withering away, and only he had the power to save her. They fought, and they squabbled until he turned them. He drained them of their elfish lives out of rage instead of pity. And when they awoke as infant vampires, their lust for their master turned to rage as well. They were driven by their newly felt thirst and raged against Dagsbrún. They blamed them for their state with one breath and begged to hunt and feed with another.

They were spiders luring their prey. They would leave the castle to stalk villages. But their favorite toy was Vandre. While he had come to the castle to serve Gammel and Dagsbrún, Vandre had ended up being the Vondod's plaything. They preyed on his weaknesses, his longing to belong, and the tragic absence of a nurturing figure in his life. Once, Dagsbrún had caught them feeding off Vandre. He had raged for days, only to be told it was he who was the villain. How could he deprive them of their one distraction? He had taken their chance to be mothers, to have homes and families. How could he deny them a boy?

And so, he turned the other way. He knew he was a monster for doing so, and he loathed himself for it. He had begged Vandre to leave, but he was fiercely loyal to the master who had given him a home, regardless of how unnatural it was. He could not understand the loyalty given to him by someone who had suffered so much because of his weakness. Nor could he understand the care given to him by Gammel.

Gammel.

His own flesh and blood, his great grandfather. When he had been a child, he idolized the elf. His magic and knowledge had filled him with wonder. But as he grew older, he realized that Gammel, despite his elvish powers, was inferior to him when it came to magic. Dagsbrún learned that he could render a human helpless by just looking at them. Indeed, some humans he could call to him with just a thought. He possessed the power to kill, control, disappear in the darkness, and become night itself. He could shift with the shadows.

And he could fly.

In truth, he despised all things about his being, except his wings Indeed, they were his vanity. Gammel had told him that not all vampires possess the ability to fly, and therefore he took pride in them. They were a connection to his father and the greatness he had possessed while living. He would often spread his wings wide and study their downy surface. Their black hue would shift to amethyst and sapphire in the candlelight. He adored the sound they made as they pierced the wind. It sounded like a gentle melody, like one his mother might have sung over his cradle. And he loved the power they possessed. They were both transportation and a tool of destruction. He could soar above the cloud and cut through an enemy with their hard edges. They were his badge, his link to his father. They were both cradle and crown to him. And yet, they were also his agony. For every time he stretched them across the heavens, it seared his body with pain.

Dagsbrún had been relatively content with his existence until the Anda had arrived on the steps of the castle. The wings that had carried him to such lofty heights seemed to pull him to the earth as she crossed the threshold to his land. He had watched her arrive with Gammel and Vandre as a hawk studies his prey. But when he tumbled to the earth, he had felt a prick in his chest he had not felt since the Vondod had arrived. It was fleeting, but the sensation stirred uncertainty in him. He had swept her up to the tower more so out of habit. His instinctual thirst had overtaken his senses, and he had had every intention of taking her life before she awoke again.

But then, Gammel had called out to him through the mists, imploring him to wait. He despised the telepathic mind games the elf would play with him, chanting with his herbs to prevent some sort of malady or catastrophe from occurring. He hated them even more because they usually worked.

He had placed her in the tower room, laying her out on the floor. Her eyes, though closed, moved uneasily beneath her eyelids, draped in downy lashes. Her hair, matted from her journey, fell across her forehead and over her ears. He noticed their pointed tips and gently curved lobes. Reaching down, he gingerly pushed her hair back behind her ears. They were elvish, but smaller and daintier than normal elf ears. He ran his finger down the curve of her neck. He could feel her blood flow in her veins. His eyes could see them glow blue under her skin. Her pulse beat under his touch, pounding against his fingers like a tribal drum.

He felt his own blood begin to warm. His thoughts began to wander as an overwhelming hunger crept through him. The walls faded, and he was in a graying wood. He lifted her into his arms, her head falling backward. Anda's body pulsated with life, with sustenance. His mind grew faint, his own body weak with hunger.

And then she moaned and turned her head toward him, her face resting against his chest. Dagsbrún jolted from his reverie and looked down. She was still unconscious but moaned as though she were in pain. He set her down on the ground once more and darted back into the shadows. He sank against the wall and watched as she pushed herself up, and Vandre and Gammel tumbled through the door. His interaction with the halfling had left him strangely confused. His instinct told him that it was natural to want to feed on her. And yet, he was hesitant. A hunter never hesitates. Or the hunter becomes the hunted.

His lack of instinct had infuriated him. It had completely thrown him off balance and stolen his keen sense of wit. Her presence set him on edge, and yet, he was drawn to her essence. With her, he found he was not stalking as though he would prey. Instead, he was pulled to her ambiance, her light emanating from her being. This had only further infuriated him because he was a thing of the shadows. To be drawn to something full of light was against his nature. It consumed him with fear—a feeling he had not felt in centuries.

When she had run off with Vandre into the woods and met the kelpie, he had known in an instant that she was in danger. He had been there to save her, even though he did not know why. He heard the screams of hapless victims at all hours of the day, yet her thoughts called loudly to them beyond any other faceless voice. He had forbidden Droime to act on his instinct because he could not understand what was happening to his own.

Gammel had said there was purpose in her presence. That their destinies were intertwined, that they had the *Förbindelse*. Dagsbrún could not even begin to understand how that could be possible. He could not touch her without wanting to consume her. To feel anything for her would be to deny his father's people… yet had his father not loved his mother? How could his darkness and her light ever coexist without consuming one another? For there was no pulse in his body except that which beat to a rhythm of rage.

He climbed the stairs to the battlements of the castle and through open the trapdoor to meet the darkened sky. The rain fell in a dark gray cascade from black clouds that blocked out the amber sun. What would irk any commoner, was a blanket of consolation for Dagsbrún. He turned his face to watch the ballet of raindrops, pirouetting from the heavens. They lovingly caressed his face with their cold touch. The wind whispered to his soul, sharing the rumblings and rumors from the clouds. The thunder rumbled over the mountains on the horizon and filled the sky with intense energy.

He heard the trapdoor crash open and whirled around, ready to strike at the intruder. Instead, he was surprised to see Anda standing there. It was evident that she had not expected anyone to be up on the battlements. She froze like a deer under the hunter's gaze, her eyes wide. Dagsbrún could see no movement, except the beating of her heart within her chest. The rain pooled on her head and cascaded down her cheekbones, to fall from her nose and lips. He was not pleased that she had invaded his solitude, nor was annoyed at her presence.

"What are you doing here?" he growled before turning back to the horizon.

"I did not think anyone would be mad enough to be up here in this storm," she replied. "Do not worry, I will go."

"No!" he whirled around to stop her. She looked at him questioningly, unsure how to respond. He lowered his voice. "I do not mind that you are here."

She took a step closer. "I do not suppose that is surprising. Considering that I am your prisoner, and therefore you minding my presence would be a bit of an oxymoron."

"A what?"

"An oxymoron. A contradiction." She looked out over the edge of the crenel to the ground below. "You will not let me leave, so it stands to reason you would not mind that I am here."

He growled. "Did your village throw you out on your ear because you talked too much?"

"My village drove me away because they feared me." She looked at him sideways. "Much like everyone fears you."

Dagsbrún shrugged. "I do not mind being feared. It gives me solitude."

"And an eternal target on your back." Anda turned and faced him. "Tell me, what is it like? Knowing you are a murderer and will live alone with your thoughts and your solitude for an eternity until someone finds a way to kill you?"

He could feel his temper boiling. "Tell me, what is like being an outcast from your home? Knowing everyone thinks you are a witch?"

She threw her hand up in anger, her veins coursing with rage. He met it with an iron grip and froze her hand in midair. The force of her swing set her off balance and threw her towards him. His grip made her knees buckle and she fell against his chest. The touch of her skin enraged her even more and she wriggled to break free of his grasp.

"Let me go," she snarled through clenched teeth.

Dagsbrún looked down at her with amusement. She could very easily be a plaything for him; a mouse to his cat. A gust of wind brought her scent to his nostrils, and he fought to repress his hunger. She smelt of honey and spice, dripping with sweetness and fire.

"Don't make it easy for me to kill," he replied. "I could kill you in an instant."

Her eyes flashed. "So I could be like one of your bloodless wraiths?" He wrenched her arm behind her back and pulled her closer. Their chins met in impassive determination—his challenging, hers defying. Their breath wafted over the surface of one another's faces as their eyes locked.

"You are an enigma," he whispered into the tresses of her hair. "You should already be dead." He forced himself to look away from the gentle curve of her neck. "All I have to do is bite."

Anda felt her body fill with a white-hot fire. She pulled back against his grip, wrenching free of all but his fingers. She could feel flames course through muscles and sinews, and watched as her body began to radiate with bluish light. Dagsbrún grimaced, and she knew that whatever she was doing was causing him pain. She smiled and twisted her arm free of his grip. Taking a step backward she sneered at him with unexpected relief and pride.

She would never quite be certain what happened next.

The earth seemed to give way under her feet, and she felt herself falling backward. She was falling downward, but she seemed to be floating, her body moving much slower than one catapulting toward certain death. So slow was her movement that simply blinking seemed to take several moments. She turned her head to one side and watched the raindrops cascade past her, wondering briefly what they were moving faster than her.

Anda was also keenly aware that she was indifferent to the act she was hurling toward her death. She questioned this, but then realized that the occurrences in her life no longer affected her. Her choices had been up to this point being burned as a witch or living as a vampire's prisoner. Death no longer seemed to be the poorest option. Closing her eyes, she saw lights float across the inky blackness. They pooled together and she could see a faint outline of her mother's face. The face smiled down at Anda with warm reassurance. Anda could feel her body warm with tender happiness.

I am coming to you, Mother.

The smile grew brighter, and she heard laughter trill across the raindrops.

Not yet, child. Not yet. Now, open your eyes.

She wished to stay lost in this reverie for eternity. But she was obedient to her mother, even after her death. And so, she opened her eyes.

He was there. How she could not fathom. But there, nonetheless. His face was only a foot away. His eyes gleamed like flint in a flame. His arms outstretched, reaching for her body as though to save her.

But how could he?

And then she heard a great rush of wind and watched, enraptured, as great black wings unfolded above him, spreading from shoulder blades. Made up of countless, glistening feathers, the wings rippled in the wind. His eyes grew brighter until they seemed to glow with the same light that had emanated from Anda.

As their eyes met, time clicked and began to move as it should, sending Anda careening toward the ground. The calm she had felt seconds before left her as death no longer gave her a sense of peace. Dagsbrún felt her panic and drove himself into the rain, stretching his fingers out to grasp her. She looked up at him, her tears mixing with the rain. She came to the realization that her final image would be his face. An even greater realization was the actuality that he was trying to save her.

Anda had nothing left. A wave of fear crashed over her and consumed her consciousness. She felt her eyes grow heavy and Dagsbrún's face began to fade away. The last thing she remembered was her body cease to fall, and his body crashed into hers.

Dagsbrún regretted his words. All of them. While his elfin half had decorum, his vampire side made him a brute. He had watched her radiate with light, elfin light, only to see the light extinguished a split second later as she stumbled over the castle wall. At that moment his rage died, and he was filled with something even more terrifying.

That he could lose her.

Fearing more thoughts like that, he dove over the side of his home after what he had thought was only a distraction. With his mind, he slowed time passing to a crawl. His chest tightened, and the muscles in his back and arms grew taught. He knew what he had to do to reach her before she was splintered to pieces on the rocks below. And he knew that doing that would hurt.

Very much.

His wings were his greatest vanity and something that he did not use often. He knew they came from his father and treasured them above anything else. But he rarely spread his wing, for the pain it caused. Each time they unfolded his flesh would shred and the bones in his body would shift to bear their weight. True, he could heal almost instantly, but not before his body went through searing agony.

She was worth the agony.

Ans so, he pushed them through his skin, spreading them to their full length and hurling himself through the rain. The rain bit at his face, but he did not care. He reached out, the sinews in his arms straining, willing his arms to grab her, but he could not.

She closed her eyes, submitting to her fate. Dagsbrún searched himself for the impossible. Just as she neared the piercing rocks. He pushed his wings forward in front of him and encompassed her in their folds. His feet and fists crashed into the earth, but she, now the only thing of value in his mind, was cradled in his wings. He sent her down gently on the ground and pulled his wings back. Arching them above her head, he made a shelter from the rain.

He pulled his knees to his chest and let the rain fall on his back. The water was a comfort to the exposed wounds on his back. He would not heal until he pulled them back, but his instinct told him to keep her dry. He knew it must be cold, but he was always cold. Still, the sensation of water trickling down his body was a comfort.

He looked down at Anda with bewilderment. What charm had this witch cast upon him? He was longing, not lustful. He wished to possess her, and yet give her everything. He craved her, and yet there was nothing he would not do to keep her from harm. She was no longer a conquest, and he could not understand it.

Except…unless…

This was forbindelse.

She moaned and turned her head restlessly. He could smell the change in her body temperature as she began to wake up, like cinnamon in a fire. He could feel himself grow restless, but he fought the urge to engulf and devour her.

Gently, he reached out and grazed the curve of her face with the tip of his wing. She leaned her head into its softness and opened her eyes.

Dagsbrún felt himself falling into those eyes. His body felt weak. He could not tell if it was her, or the fact that he was unsure when the last time he had fed was. His mouth was dry, his mind a myriad of colors and flashes of light.

He leaned towards her and managed what he felt was a smile. "Hello."

Chapter 10

Her first thought was that death was mocking her. For her captor had pursued her even into the afterlife. He hovered over her like a vulture waiting for its prey to perish. Slowly, her mind cleared, and sensation returned to her body, and she realized that she was still very much alive. Her back and head throbbed with a steady, painful beat, and the world tilted on its axis, causing her to feel as though she were still plummeting into oblivion.

And then he spoke.

"Hello."

His voice sounded far away as it echoed across her mind. But she knew he was beside her because his breath cascaded over her skin like a summer breeze. She moaned and forced herself to sit up, only to fall back once more. This time the earth was replaced with something soft. Through hazy eyes, she saw that he had caught her with one of his wings.

And then, she remembered the wings. Wings piercing the air to pull her from certain death. Wings attached to the being, the creature that was trying to save her. They were soft, like the folds of a feather bed. Silky, like the plumage of a pheasant. And yet, they belonged to *him*.

She groaned and pushed herself to her feet, determined to walk away on her own. Her pulsing head confused her thoughts.

How could she thank her captor? She would not be in this position at all if it were not for him. Her feet crossed over one another, struggling to make even contact with the ground. She was uncertain of which direction they should even take her. The castle? The forest? Her village?

All seemed to lead to her demise.

"Wait!"

His voice seemed closer now.

"Please," she sighed. "Do not help me anymore."

He cut her off. "You should rest. You just fell to what should have been your death."

She pushed past him. "And I suppose I should be thanking you?"

Dagsbrún smirked. "It would be the courteous thing to do."

Her temper mixed with her pounding head made it even more impossible to walk and therefore made her more infuriated still. "Letting me die would have been the courteous thing to do!" She stormed toward the castle. "Now I am right back where I began. Shunned by my people and imprisoned by a narcissistic monster!"

He did not care if had tried to save her life, her wounds wounded him. "Witch!" he yelled.

She froze mid-stride and whirled around. "Beast!" she screamed. He exasperated her, standing there with his wings still unfurled, looking as though he were her savior. She took a step towards him. "You should have done me the courtesy of keeping your wings… wherever it is you keep them and stayed atop your castle. You do not need to brandish them about on my behalf."

A cloud passed over his face. "It was not brandishing. It was benevolence." He walked towards her slowly, and as he did, he pulled his wings inward. "Every time I release them, it tears my flesh. It breaks my bones. And still, I spread them. For you. I caught you inches from being scattered on the rock. Even then, I could have put them back, but I did not. I sheltered you from the rain, which was a waste because we are both now drenching ourselves." He stopped inches from her face. "Do not insult me by saying I brandished my wings. They tear me from the inside out. Every. Single. Time."

Water cascaded down his forehead, collected on his nose, and dripped down onto her lips. She licked it away, feeling its iciness on her tongue. "I am sorry," she whispered.

His face softened. "My wings are not something I take lightly. Not all of us have them, but my father did. In a way, they were his gift to me."

Anda felt a twinge of guilt. "I suppose I should apologize for being such a burden." She smiled wryly. "Perhaps if you would let me go, you would no longer feel the need to protect your conquest."

"He cannot let you go."

They both turned to see Gammel standing under the castle's arches. He had pulled the hood of his cloak over his head, and so his face was shielded from them. But they could see his eyes, glimmering in the torchlight.

"Cannot?" Anda shouted through the rain. "Or will not?"

Gammel left the shelter of arches, walking towards them. "He cannot. Forces have been set in motion that bind you to us. To him."

She wiped away the rain. "What forces?"

"Forces beyond what you could possibly imagine. Forces beyond this world."

"Rubbish," she scoffed.

Gammel removed his cloak and placed it around her shoulders. "Let us get you inside. While he cannot grow cold, you are still half-human." He led the way back up the path.

"What forces?" she persisted.

"You best tell her, old man," Dagsbrún snickered. "And you better give her something believable."

Anda glared and Dagsbrún. "I find it increasingly easy to believe in almost anything."

Gammel ignored their sparring. "This world and the world beyond the Vale are linked like strands on a spider's web. It is known as Gréasáin. Damage one strand, the rest will be susceptible to destruction."

"I still do not understand how this pertains to me."

"These strands are the balance upon which we so precariously tread. Upset the balance, you upset the journey."

"What you are saying," Dagsbrún interjected, "Is that the balance is upset?"

Gammel nodded. "It has been for millennia. And like a worm, it has slowly chewed away at an apple already rotten, until now, we are clinging to what is left of the core."

Dagsbrún pushed open the door to the castle. "What caused this decay?"

"The age-old battle between elf and vampire. They have all but destroyed one another. And their actions have spilled over into this world."

They entered Dagsbrún's library and Anda sank into a chair in front of the fire. "I and I suppose you think I possess the power to stop the world from complete annihilation."

Gammel's gaze was unwavering. "I do not think it. I know it."

Dagsbrún shut the door. "You cannot possibly be serious. She has no skill. Her power, the little she has, is wild and unruly. She has no means to save this world or the Vale."

Gammel turned and fixed his eyes on Dagsbrún. "Perhaps you are concerned for her well-being?"

Dagsbrún grimaced. "Hardly." He crossed the floor to the table. "I am more concerned with what will happen to my prisoner if you make her our liberator."

Anda scowled at him. "The only thing I wish to liberate you from is your pitiful existence."

Dagsbrún could feel his temper flare. "You could not so much as liberate an egg from a chicken!"

Gammel slammed his staff into the floor. "Enough!" The room echoed in the silence that followed. His eyes sparked in the light from the fire. "I have been alive longer than your small minds could even fathom. And never, in all the centuries of watching elves and vampires fight with one another have I ever seen such absurd behavior." He set himself gingerly into the chair opposite Anda. "You must find a way to reconcile. And Anda," he leaned across and gripped her hand. "You must learn to believe in what you are capable of."

Anda knew she could not win this argument. But she could not fathom what lay ahead of her. Did she possess some sort of magic? She supposed so. Though why it chose to run through her veins, she did not know. And just what she could do with it was beyond her realm of understanding. How could she, a half-breed from a tiny village, change the course of this world, and what lay beyond?

She looked over at Dagsbrún, leaning carelessly against the great table. Why must he play a part in all of this? He, with his cocky demeanor and smug demeanor expressions. He, with his sapphire eyes and spectral complexion.

She snapped her gaze away and looked back at Gammel. "Clearly, I have no choice. I hope you have a plan on how to make me this hero you speak of."

Dagsbrún leapt from the table. "You do not propose to go through with this?" He looked at them incredulously. "Gammel, you will be responsible for her death!"

"Perhaps not. She simply needs a push to spread her wings."

Dagsbrún could not fully process her decision. His feelings were conflicted within him. Why should he care what her demise would be beyond these walls? And yet, he felt his whole being constricted with fear, a feeling that until now was completely foreign to him. But why he was afraid, he could not understand. He was a transcendent being, with powers that were unmatched. The lack of a heart made him invulnerable. He could take life without a care or second thought. In fact, he thrived off it. But the thought of Anda facing unimaginable forces made him feel entirely helpless. And that feeling of helplessness sent him near to the edge of madness.

He breathed deeply, trying to control his emotions. "If you are to train Anda, then I expect to be there." He stood behind her chair. "You said it yourself, Gammel. We both are bound to this mission. I need to understand the power necessary to restore peace."

Gammel smiled. "You misunderstand me, Dagsbrún. *She* is the power. You must protect her."

Anda scowled. "He is supposed to protect me?"

Gammel nodded. "I think he is off to an admiral start, don't you think? Saving you from crashing on the rocks? It's not every day a vampire saves its intended meal."

"It was reactionary," Dagsbrún mumbled.

Gammel chuckled. "Nothing reactionary about it." He pulled himself up with his staff. "Now, if the both of you are done quibbling, we will begin."

"Now?" Anda asked.

Gammel crossed to the door and threw it open. "Now."

Anda stood to her feet and moved to follow him, but Dagsbrún gripped her arm. She looked up at him. His eyes were tinged with feeling, something she had not expected to see. She tried to speak, but her throat seemed filled with feelings of her own. "Let go of me," she whispered.

"Anda, this is a death wish."

She wrenched free of his grasp. "Perhaps death would be a welcome adventure." She turned and followed after Gammel.

Dagsbrún listened to her footsteps as they faded down the hallway, envisioning all the cruel deaths that could befall her. As they grew more distant, panic overpowered him, and he hurried after them into the shadows.

Gammel led them out to the same clearing Vandre had taken Anda. The heavens drew back the rain, but the clouds remained foreboding. The wind was not so gracious and swirled about in the grasses and through the trees. The elf drove his staff into the ground and drew a large circle.

"This," he said gesturing in a wide arc, "Is your training ground. And you will not leave it until I am satisfied."

Anda placed her foot inside the circle. "What does that mean?"

"Satisfied means that I approve."

Dagsbrún brushed passed her. "You cannot possibly expect her to remain out here in the wind and the rain.?"

"If you would open your eyes as much as you open your mouth, you would see that the rain has stopped. And the wind will aid in our lessons."

Anda pulled the cloak Gammel had given her tightly around her body. "How could it possibly help?"

Gammel stood in the middle of the circle and gestured to Anda to join him. "As I have said, all things in this world are connected. What affects one thing, affects another. The wind blows through a tree causing a leaf to fall. The leaf drifts down to the water and creates a ripple." He wrapped his hands tightly around his staff. "In the same way, we can learn to control the effect the way which our surroundings impact our existence." He raised his staff above his head and in a great booming voice that echoed from the castle walls to the mountains beyond the forest he shouted, *"Quildë?"* The wind instantly softened to a small breeze, moving only the tips of the grass.

Dagsbrún chuckled. "I can do that simply by looking at someone."

Gammel scowled at him. "Yes, but not everyone has that power. Nor does everyone wish to silence their meal before partaking of it." He turned to Anda. "Come, it is your turn."

Anda took a step back. "Mine?"

Gammel stood behind her and gently gripped her arms. "Close your eyes," he whispered. "See the wind in your mind. What does it look like?"

Anda laughed. "Look like? One cannot see the wind."

"Try."

Anda squeezed her eyes shut. Searching beyond the blackness for what Gammel spoke of. She felt as though she were spiraling downward, sinking into herself, searching the chasm of her own body for answers. And then, from off in the blackened distance, she saw a spark of blue light. It grew and shifted into a small flourish, swirling, and twisting its way toward her.

"I see it," she gasped.

"Good!" Gammel took a step back. "Now, call it to you."

"How do I do that?"

---

[2] Quildë means "quiet" in Elvish.

Gammel smiled. "Search yourself. You already know the answer."

Anda sighed. How did one call the wind? It was not an animal to be called with a whistle, nor was it a human to be ushered with a wave of her arm. She could feel herself grow agitated, and the flurry of wind began to fade. Panic rose within her, and she cried out silently in her mind, begging the wind not to go.

And the wind heard her.

It flowed over the ground in rippling waves toward her. She reached her arms out towards it, and it swirled about her in a myriad of blue hues. She could feel it course through her body, a warm westerly wind warming every part of her from her fingers to the tips of her ears. She could hear it dance through the trees and write poetry with its breath in the skies.

"Gammel," she whispered with wonder. "Gammel, I have it."

The old elf beamed. "Now, use it."

Anda drew a deep breath and pulled her arms close to her chest. She opened her eyes and searched for a target. Her mouth turned up as she smiled. With a shout of determination, she threw her arms in the direction of a slender tree several hundred yards away. A roaring gust hurled across the ground and swept up and over the tree, ripping branches and leaves from the trunk. When it settled, the tree was a mere stick protruding from the earth.

Everything was silent, except for the sound of Anda's deep breathing. The air grew heavy and dense, saturated with the presence of magic. Anda gasped and looked at Gammel, hoping he approved. He pushed his gray locks from his face and nodded his approval.

"Again," he ordered.

"Now wait!" Dagsbrún held up his hand. "That is more than any elf has done on their first try. You cannot expect her to do more."

Gammel pushed him away with the tip of his staff. "We have an intolerable shortage of time, Dagsbrún."

"We will have all the time in the world if she destroys herself!"

"We will all be destroyed if she does not learn!" Gammel slammed his staff into the ground, causing it to rupture. "Do you not understand, boy?"

Dagsbrún's face grew hard. "Do not call me boy, old man."

"If Anda does not learn to control her power, the Vale will fall. Vampires will destroy Elf, and then they will come here and destroy this world. Everything that your parents fought to create will be for nothing!"

"Tread carefully when speaking about my parents."

"I have more right to speak of them, especially your mother. The same fate will befall Anda if either humans or vampires get to her before you can mend things."

Anda threw up her hands. "You keep speaking of "us" and "we." Just what is it we are supposed to do?"

Gammel sighed. "You must go to the source of the chaos."

"What do you mean?"

Dagsbrún laughed. "He wants us to go to the Vale."

Anda took a step back. "Why?"

Gammel leaned heavily on his staff. "Because it is the only way. The elders must see that there are two halflings that have the potential to do good, to mend the wounds caused by battles so old no one remembers why they were begun in the first place. If the two of you can find peace with one another, then there is a small chance that peace can be made in the Vale."

Anda looked from Gammel to Dagsbrún. Their eyes both told her how necessary it was that she succeed. She had just stripped a tree with the wind, what could possibly go wrong? She straightened her shoulders, crossed back to the center of the circle, and held her hands upward. She looked at Gammel and asked,

"What next?"

High above her training, three figures watched Anda with keen interest. Morsdog, Gudinne, and Sybil observed Anda control the wind, eyes wide with desire.

"She has the gift!" Morsdog hissed.

"Her power will destroy home!" Sybil moaned. She turned to Gudinne who watched Anda through slanted eyes. "What do we do?"

"She will steal him from us!" Morsdog wailed.

"Silence!" Gudinne screamed at the other two. They shrank back into a corner and wrapped their arms and legs around one another. Gudinne turned back to the scene below. "She will not steal Dagsbrún from us."

"But what will we do?" Sybil shrieked.

Gudinne leaned against the window frame. "We will wait. We will wait until the old elfish fool teaches her all his secrets. We will wait until she is in full possession of her power."

"And then?" Morsdog licked her lips in anticipation.

"Then we strike. We strike fast and we strike hard. We drink her dry and Dagsbrún will be unable to resist us."

"And what if she is more powerful than you?

The Vondod turned toward the direction of a voice speaking out within the shadows. Vandre materialized and stumbled toward them. He was pale and unsteady, his arms and neck marked bites. He stopped in front of the window and looked down.

Gudinne pushed him to one side. "Stupid boy."

Vandre chuckled. "Smart enough to bring her here. Smart enough to recognize her power is going to destroy you."

Gudinne grabbed him by the neck and lifted him off the floor. "Silence, boy!" She flashed her teeth and chuckled. "I could break your skinny neck and drain you dry in the blink of an eye."

"And I will gladly die knowing that your fate at Dagsbrún's hands will be much worse than my own demise." He pried her fingers from his neck and fell to the ground. "I may be your plaything. I am not your meal."

Gudinne shrieked and dragged her long nails across the stone walls. "Curse you! Curse Dagsbrún!"

Vandre stumbled back to the window. "Curse all you want. Your downfall has come to Castle Skog. It is raw. And it is radiant.

Chapter 11

Gammel held true to his word. Anda did not leave the circle. She stayed there, and she learned. She learned to command the elements—wind, fire, water, and earth. She learned herbology—how to use cloves to heal, and thyme to protect. She learned how to use the power of the moon and radiate the power of the sun.

When she was not harnessing her power, she learned the art of defense. Dagsbrún taught her swordsmanship. While his two-handed sword was too heavy for her, he gave her a smaller broadsword to practice with. They weaved and lunged around the circle, contracting toward one another, and then pushing away.

And when Anda's legs gave way and she collapsed on the cold earth, Dagsbrún would sit beside her in silence. They did not speak, and rarely did they make eye contact. But he would not leave her side. She convinced herself that he was guarding his property, and yet, there were moments when she questioned her own convictions. Moments when he would think she was not watching, and she would catch him looking at her. Not with the gaze of a predator, but rather with the look of a protector. His eyes were soft and calm, like the sea in the morning light. Anda found herself sinking into them and battling to not drown. She found that when she was not learning to control the elements or wield a sword, she was fighting against herself.

When they did talk, she would find that the words coming out of her mouth were spiteful, yet her heart found itself craving his conversation. She found that she would challenge him simply so they could argue. In truth, though she would never admit it, his presence gave her the drive to push through all that Gammel threw her way.

A week went by and still, Anda had not left the circle. On the seventh day, Gammel appeared in the middle of sword practice. He motioned for them to stop, and they lowered their swords.

"The time has come for you to accomplish your last task."

Anda set her sword against a rock. "And then I may leave the circle?"

Gammel nodded. "Leave the circle and the castle."

"What do I need to do?"

Gammel sat down on a boulder. "Elves like you are not meant to roam alone. And therefore, it is time for you to choose a familiar."

Anda blinked. "A Familiar?"

"An animal companion. One that was made to be your protector."

Dagsbrún interjected. "Now wait a moment. I thought I was meant to be the brawn on this quest. Why does she need a Familiar?"

"Because, despite what your arrogant mind thinks, you are not without weaknesses. And in the Vale, Anda will need all the protection we can give her." Gammel turned back to Anda. "And so, for your last task, you will choose your Familiar."

"How?"

"Call to it."

"Call to it?" Anda could not imagine how to call something she did not even know.

Gammel nodded. "In the same way you have learned to summon the elements. If you call your Familiar, they will come to you."

Anda turned from Gammel and Dagsbrún and crossed to the center of the circle. Here she had stood for the last seven days and become someone she had never expected to be. Here she had pushed beyond the limits the world had given her and become more than even she herself understood. Now her final task was to call an animal as her father would call his livestock.

"It is a noble task," Gammel interrupted her thoughts as though he could read them. "It is no common beast that you summon."

She shut her eyes and dove down into herself once more. This time, the expanse before her was void of any life or movement. She retreated into her mind and searched out the creature that she was to call hers. The ground began to move and shift like sand blowing in the desert. Mists rose in the darkness and surrounded Anda in a dappled blanket. She let herself be embraced by mists and drift through her own mind.

And then, through the mists, she saw a shape form in the distance. It shifted and moved with the swirling of the mists. She looked harder and saw the shape materialize into that of a great, black horse. Its nostrils flared as its hot breath melted into the air around it. Its hooves struck the ground, causing bits of gravel and rocks to fly. The creature's coat was obsidian black and so smooth that it glistened as it moved over the horse's muscular form. Anda was awestruck by the sheer power and beauty of it. But as the creature drew nearer, she felt a sense of dread well up within her.

Dagsbrún saw her take a step backward and realized the source of her fear. He looked across the circle at Gammel, who appeared completely unmoved. "Are you mad!" he shouted to the elf. "It will kill her!"

"It must be done!" Gammel yelled back.

Dagsbrún bounded to Anda's side. Racing toward her was none other than the kelpie, Droime, who had tried to drag her to her death. He stood behind Anda and gently whispered into her ear, trying not to let his voice convey his own fear. "Anda, can you hear me?"

"What do I do?" she whispered through clenched teeth. "It will kill me."

"There is one way to stop it," he replied. "One way to command a kelpie."

"How?"

"You must grab his bridle. Grab it and do not let go."

Anda heard his instructions but could not convey them to her body. She was completely frozen. Her reflexes that had been so conditioned refused to act.

Dagsbrún sensed this. If he did not help her, Droime would destroy her. He reached out and gripped her arm. Slowly he ran his hand down to her hand and turned it palm upward, spreading her fingers out.

"Do you trust me?" he whispered.

"Never," she hissed.

He smiled. "Well, I suppose this will be your last lesson with Gammel and the first lesson in trusting me." He gripped her hand and held it out.

"What are you doing?" she yelled. She could feel the ground shake as Droime thundered towards them. She shrank back against Dagsbrún, the icy coldness of his skin sent shock waves through her body.

Dagsbrún felt her fear and pulled her closer, trying to ignore how much he craved her. "Steady," he whispered in her ear.

Droime careened towards them. His eyes afire, his hooves carving up the earth. Dagsbrún body went rigid, holding up Anda who felt her legs crumbling beneath her. Droime reared up on his hind legs and let a piercing whinny. As his front legs came back down to the earth, Dagsbrún lifted Anda off the ground, throwing her toward the kelpie's head. Anda opened her eyes and saw Droime's mane shining bright against his dark coat. She stretched her fingers out and gripped it firmly in her hands. The force of Droime's speed tossed her onto his back as they careened past Dagsbrún and Gammel.

"Pull his head back!" Dagsbrún shouted.

All her breath had left her body, and the land sped by her as she fought to hold on. Anda pulled with all her might to slow Droime down. Wrenching back with all her might, she pulled the kelpie's head back. He reared up, his legs pawing at the air and then came down with a thunderous crash.

Anda did not know what her hot breath against the cold air was, and what was the dust that Droime had kicked up. She clung to the bridle, afraid to let go and have him take off with her once more. He turned and looked up at her, his eyes now void of fire.

You have bested me.

Anda heard the kelpie's voice in her head. "That was not my intention."

You have my bridle and my service.

Anda inhaled deeply. "I thank you," she whispered. "Now, with your permission, I would like to get down."

Droime tossed his head. *There is no need to ask. My magic no longer has power over you. You have tamed me.*

Anda dismounted and gently ran her fingers through his mane. "Perhaps, we can let one another remain as we are, neither conquering the other. Perhaps together, we can run wild."

Droime nickered softly and touched his nose to her forehead, and Anda knew she had made a friend.

She heard yelling behind her and turned to see Dagsbrún and Gammel rushing towards them. Gammel reached her first, enveloping her in an overwhelming bear hug. He swung her around, his deep laugh echoing across the fields. Setting her down, he gently cupped her chin and brought her eyes up to meet his. They twinkled with approval, surrounded by laugh lines.

"Well done, halfling," he beamed. "Well done!"

Dagsbrún came up behind them, relief etched across his face. He reached out to embrace Anda but pulled back and instead offered only his hand. "You did it. You should be immensely proud."

Anda gingerly took his hand, feeling his frigid touch once more. "Thank you," she muttered.

Gammel laughed once more. "You *both* should be proud."

Dagsbrún let go of her hand. "It was all her. I did nothing."

"On the contrary," Anda replied. "I would be dead under Droime's hooves were it not for you."

Gammel put an arm around each of their shoulders. "You worked together, combining your strength. That is precisely what you needed to do. And now," he turned and patted Droime's neck, "with the help of this kelpie, you have a fighting chance." He chuckled. "Though I did not have such a powerful beast picked out for you."

Anda smiled. "Nor was it my intention."

Droime whinnied and tossed his head. He nuzzled Anda's shoulder and then turned and galloped off into the forest.

"Where is he going?" Anda asked.

Gammel turned back toward the castle. "He will come when he is needed. You two are bound together now."

Anda followed him. "Now that I have a kelpie at my beck and call, might I sleep in a bed tonight?"

Gammel chuckled. "Come. Food, fire, and a warm bed are waiting for you."

Dagsbrún watched them walk away and was left wondering if he would ever be able to come to terms with the myriad of emotions coursing through his veins. She had entered his lands a wild and wayward girl and in just a few short weeks had become a force to be reckoned with. She drove him mad, and yet there was none other he strove so hard to curb his instincts for. She would be the death of him.

Or his deliverance.

Chapter 12

The castle was draped in silence that night. All the inhabitants had drifted to their corners to recover and make ready for what was to come next. Gammel had locked himself away with his potions and text, while Dagsbrún retreated to the tower. The halls and rooms were silent, everything holding its breath in restless anticipation.

Anda had returned to her room to find a tub filled with water, the fire lit, and the bed sheets turned down. She removed her dirtied and bloodied clothes and sank into the soothing waters. Adrenalin drained from her body only to be replaced with pain and fatigue. The water caressed the surface of her skin and gently washed away the grime. Her body was buoyant and light, momentarily free of any burden, and she was very conscious of how wonderful it felt.

Sinking deeper, she covered all but her nose with water. Her mind was floating now... drifting over a plane of oblivion. All that existed was shadow and silence. Gammel had taught her how to empty her mind of everything so that she would fill it with whatever she desired, and she found that she quite delighted in this. For in this, she could control not only her emotions but her thoughts.

And in this state, her thoughts drifted through the castle to Dagsbrún's tower. In her mind's eye, the stairs materialized for her to climb to his door. It was ajar and she pushed it open.

He was there.

There in a worn and rugged chair, his legs stretched out across an animal skin rug. He had removed his shirt and his skin shone in the firelight. Anda was struck by how the moving light accentuated his form. His arms and chest rose and fell in valleys and summits of shadow. His face, half-hidden in the darkness, was sculptured marble, smooth and hard. It was turned away from her, his eyes gazing out the window, wandering in his own mind.

Anda forgot to breathe. He was so magnificent he was sitting there like a statue frozen in place. He was terrifyingly beautiful. She knew that she should turn and leave, but she could not pull her eyes away. He was danger incarnate, and being in his presence greatly increased her chance of death. After all, that was what he was. A hunter who mesmerized his prey before destroying them.

And yet, he had not destroyed her. She was sure he had come close. She had felt his breath on her neck more than once, and still, he had saved her more than once. And that thought—that he was created to destroy but had only ever protected her—created immense confusion in her mind.

As she watched him, he shifted and turned his head toward her. Somewhere in the back of her mind, she knew this was all in her head, but she still took a step back. He pushed himself up from the chair and crossed the room, his face void of all expression.

Anda.

She heard his voice but could not understand how he could see her. She took another step back.

Anda.

Suddenly, Anda was not as certain as she had been that she had manifested this meeting in her mind.

Anda. Dagsbrún reached out to her.

Anda gasped and sat up in the bathtub, water cascading over the edge and falling to the floor. She pushed her hair back and wiped her face, her heart pounding in her chest. She was alone, back in her room, and yet, she still looked over her shoulder—imagining he would be standing there, draped in shadows. But there was no one. The room was empty and silent.

And then, *Anda*.

This time, it came from far away. He was calling to her. She pulled herself out of the tub and wrapped herself in a dressing gown. Water collected at her feet as she strode across the floor toward the door. She pushed the door open, its aged hinges creaking and echoing down the hall.

Anda. His voice was filled with urgency.

She followed the sound of his voice through the corridors, filled with both fear and longing. There was no sound, except the occasional call of his voice.

Anda.

Turning down an unlit hallway, she realized she did not remember this part of the castle and wondered if she had never been there. The doors were covered in dust and appeared to have not been open in quite some time. Tapestries that had been worn thin years ago hung in tatters, making a poor attempt to cover the paneled walls.

Anda.

His voice came from a door at the end of the hall, the only door that was ajar. She pushed the door open further and stepped in. It was dark and smelt of age and decay. Crossing the dust-ridden floor, she looked for any sign of movement. He must be here.

"Dagsbrún?" She sensed movement behind her, the slightest rush of wind. Turning, she was the myriad of cobwebs swaying. "Hello?"

Like curtains, the cobwebs parted, and three shadowy figures stepped into the dim light.

The Vondod.

"Hello, child," Morsdog hissed, her sharp teeth protruding from her mouth.

Anda's heart leaped into her throat. Now it all became clear. She had not heard Dagsbrún's voice, he had heard theirs. Using their trickery, they had lured her here.

Gudinne stepped in front of the other two. "Foolish elf. Did you think he was calling you? Why would he want someone like you?"

Anda swallowed. "He is the master of this castle. When he calls, I obey."

Sybil cackled. "Come now. We are all women here. And we can see your thoughts. We all know why you came."

Anda now felt she was on borrowed time. "And why is that?"

Gudinne walked behind her. She picked a lock of Anda's hair and twisted it around her finger. "Because," she whispered with a hiss. "Because you want him." She pulled hard on Anda's hair, and Anda fell against the Vondod. The wraith wrapped her arm tightly around Anda's throat and squeezed.

"Did you think we would let you steal him?" Sybil snickered.

"He is our life source. Our love." Morsdog whimpered. "He is not meant for you."

Despite her predicament, Anda felt her temper flare. "That is most amusing. He seems to think you are three thorns in his side."

Gudinne squeezed her arm tighter. "As my sister said, he is not meant for you. But you," she bit her lip, "you are meant for us."

Anda knew she was losing. "I do not think so. I prefer to congregate with the living."

Gudinne screamed and threw her captive to the floor. "We will not be mocked!" She slashed her long fingers across Anda's face, leaving deep gashes. "We have watched you this last week, biding our time." She crouched down. "We have watched all that lovely magic bubble to the service. And now... now we will have it."

"Drain her!" Morsdog screamed.

Gudinne hissed. "Not yet!" She turned back to Anda. "First, I want to be able to say your goodbyes."

"I have no one to say goodbye to," Anda panted.

Gudinne chuckled. "On the contrary." She turned toward the shadows. "Come out."

Anda searched the darkness, wondering who could possibly be watching. The cobwebs shifted and the figure of Vandre materialized. She gasped. His face was a ghostly white and his arms riddled with bite marks. His eyes sank deep into his head and stared at her with shallow, sad eyes.

Sybil grabbed him, dragging him to Anda's side. "Say hello, Vandre."

"Hello," he whimpered.

Anda felt her heart sink. "What have they done to you?"

"He is our morsel," Gudinne lifted Vandre's chin. "A gift. From Dagsbrún."

Anda pushed herself up. "I do not believe it!" She looked at Vandre. "Vandre, is it true?"

Vandre lowered his eyes. "It does not matter what is and isn't true."

Anda reached out and gripped his arm. "The truth always matters. Who did this to you?"

Before he could answer, Gudinne pulled her back. She ran a razor-sharp fingernail along the curve of Anda's throat. "Vandre has been but a tidbit, a light bite to tide us over. You, my dear, will be our feast. And when we have consumed your power, we will conquer Dagsbrún, and he... he will serve us."

Anda cringed. It all became clear to her. The Vondod meant to kill her and consume her powers. It made sense. She had not been aware of her powers because they had been buried deep within her until Gammel had taught her how to manifest and control them. Now they flowed just beneath the surface of her skin, easily reachable by the three wraiths. With her power, they would then take on Dagsbrún... and in all likeliness, win. And then, who knew how far their depravity would spread? Gammel, Vandre, Castle Skog, the village, her family... they would all be destroyed. And after, they would take on the Vale. There would be no hope for peace.

"You mean to rule the world," she gasped.

Gudinne laughed. "This world, and all others."

Anda laughed. "Both? That is a lot for three vampires. Aren't you being a bit egotistical?"

"We will populate the world with new vampires, more powerful than the ones living now," Sybil murmured, lost in her own reverie.

Anda coughed under the pressure of Gudinne's body on her own. "Again, with the ego. Who would have you?"

Sybil sailed across the room and slammed her fist into Anda's face. "Then we will kill them!" she shrieked. "We will kill them all!"

Morsdog hobbled forward. "Come, we are wasting time." Let us be done with her." She pushed Sybil to the side. "I want the first bite!"

Sybil hissed at Morsdog. "Get in line, hag! I am going first!"

Gudinne swiped at both and pulled Anda up against her chest. "I planned all this, I get the first bite,"

Morsdog growled. "Go on then. Get on with it!"

Gudinne pulled Anda's neck toward her mouth. "Shame Dagsbrún never bit you. This is truly going to be unpleasant for you."

Anda turned her head toward Vandre, who was slumped in a corner. She tried to smile at him, but fear froze her face. Vandre understood her intention though and shook his head. Pushing himself up, he mouthed the words, "He is coming."

She managed the smallest of smiles as Gudinne drove her teeth into Anda's neck. Pain seared through her entire body as her flesh felt as though it were ignited in flame. She could see Gudinne's thoughts, her visions of a world laid to waste, covered in shadow and ash. And yet, Vandre had told he would come. He would stop the pain.

But where was he?

Her mind began to drift backwards. Back to being afraid in the forest. Back home to her father's face. Back to her birth and her mother's smile. Back to when she was nothing but a thought floating in oblivion. Somewhere in her head, it occurred to her that it was odd she should be so at peace as she faced certain death.

And then, a great whirlwind flew into the room. She was hurled against the wall, her body crashing into the stone and crumbling. Semi-conscious she peered through heavy eyelids. and saw that the other inhabitants of the room had been tossed about as well. Vandre was unmoving in the same corner he had been in, and the Vondod lay in a pile in the middle of the room. They stirred and stood, seemingly disoriented, and confused as to what had knocked them to the ground.

"You fools!"

The voice rained down from the rafters and from within the walls. Morsdog cowered, Sybil burst into tears, and Gudinne appeared mildly uncertain as to what she should now do. And then, appearing as though he were made of nothing but air, Dagsbrún materialized in the doorway. His face was lined with rage and his eyes flashed his fury.

"Dagsbrún!" Gudinne smiled, but her voice cracked. "We were just speaking about you."

"Have you gone completely mad?" He roared. He grabbed Sybil and hurled her to the ground. "You had little sense when you came here, but it is clear to me all sanity has left your empty souls."

"We were saving her for you, Master," Morsdog groveled. "She was trying to kill Vandre."

"Yes, yes!" Sybil pushed herself up. "But we stopped her!"

"Lies!" Dagsbrún screamed. "Do not take me for a fool!"

Gudinne came up behind him and wrapped her arms around his chest. "Dear Dagsbrún," she whispered. "Do not be angry with us. We were only trying to save the poor boy."

"Save him!" Dagsbrún wrenched himself free and strode to Vandre. He held up one of the boy's arms. "His arms are decked in your salvation!"

"We were hungry!" Sybil cried.

Dagsbrún grabbed her by the hair. "You three came to me, and I, like an arrogant fool, made you what you are. But you have repeatedly disobeyed me. You have a choice: to live with your circumstances or wallow in it. You have wallowed. And it has turned you into abusers and murderers."

Gudinne let out a maniacal laugh. "You think you have a right to say that to us? You, the king hunter? Tell me, how many innocent lives have you taken?"

"I live with what I do," Dagsbrún replied. "It haunts me. He touched his forehead to Sybil's. "You haunt me." He let go of her hair and turned to Gudinne. "And this is why you will leave this place. Tonight."

The room fell silent. The Vondod stared at him. Sybil shrank against Gudinne's skirts. Gudinne reached down and touched her head. "You cannot be serious."

"I am most serious," he replied evenly. "You were going to kill her. Take her power and then use it to kill me." He pushed Gudinne toward the window. "You disobeyed me. You would have created a complete wasteland with your lust for power. So, you will leave. You will wander. You will starve, and you will suffer."

Gudinne swallowed. "Or?"

Dagsbrún gave her a small smile. "Or I will lock you in a room and set it on fire, and you will burn until you are nothing but ash."

Gudinne bit her lip. "I curse you!" She screamed in his face.

He smiled. "I have been cursed since birth." He gestured to Morsdog and Sybil. "It is time for you to leave my home."

The Vondod scurried onto the window ledge and huddled together. Gudinne wrapped her arms around the other two wraiths. "We will haunt you, Dagsbrún. We will come to you in your nightmares and never let you rest!"

Dagsbrún was unmoving. "Except I do not sleep. Now, jump."

Wailing, the Vondod turned and faced the night. Gudinne gripped her sister's hand and whispered, "Together, forever." She then leaped from the window, pulling them with her. They hurdled for several feet before disappearing into the fog. Dagsbrún continued to watch and a few moments later three black ravens soared through the clouds, shrieking as they flew toward the horizon.

He sighed and leaned heavily against the window ledge. Anda moaned and he turned towards her. She was wounded, but she would live. He knelt beside her and gently pulled her head onto his lap. He turned his head to examine Gudinne's bite on her neck. He touched it gently and muttered, "Helbrede[3]."

The mark slowly scabbed over and then the scar disappeared. Dagsbrún breathed a sigh of relief and pulled her close. "Do not worry," he whispered. "I have you."

---

[3] Helbrede means "cure" in Danish.

Chapter 13

Dagsbrún carried Anda to her room and stayed with her through the night, watching over her from a chair in the corner. She tossed in her bedsheets, but he was confident she would heal. And yet, anxiety poured over him in waves. He remained unmoving as he watched her with unblinking eyes.

In the morning when the sun streamed in, Anda turned toward the light and opened her eyes. Her mind was hazy for a moment and then the events of the night came pouring back to her. She sat up in bed, looking around wildly.

"They are gone."

She turned toward the voice and saw Dagsbrún rise from his chair and cross to her bed. Sinking back onto the pillows, she let out a long sigh. "I feel perfectly dreadful."

He smiled. "The Vondod were out for blood. But I made them leave. They will not harm you again." He brushed a strand of hair behind her ear. "They will be more concerned with surviving on their own."

She remembered Gudinne's bite and reached up to touch her neck. "Gudinne. She bit me. I felt as though I were burning alive. But..."

"There is no wound." Dagsbrún stood and crossed to the window. "Apparently you are full of surprises. Your elf blood is stronger than I think even Gammel realizes. You healed..."

Anda blinked. "I healed myself?"

He nodded. "With a bit of help from me. You continue to be full of surprises." He looked out the window. "It will be a nice asset for you to store away in case you ever face another adversary."

She swung her feet over the bed and stood. "If?" She crossed to the looking glass and studied her face and neck. "If Gammel has his way, I will end the war. I cannot imagine that will be done peacefully."

Dagsbrún nodded. "That would be a bit dull."

Anda looked at him in the looking glass's reflection. She remembered the Vondod, even Vandre, but she could not remember how she had returned to her room. "Just what are you doing here?"

He turned from the window. "What do you mean?"

Anda turned from the looking glass. "I remember following your voice, except it was not you, it was the Vondod. I remember seeing Vandre and being bitten, but you were not there. Vandre said you were coming, but I only remember the wind. A huge gust of wind. And now I am here, as are you. But where were you last night? When Vandre needed you. When I needed you."

His smile slowly faded. "While I have immense power, the Vondod used theirs to block my site. Had I known, you know I would have come."

Anda raised an eyebrow. "Would you?"

Her tone threw him off guard. "I would have been there in an instant. I wish you could believe that."

She turned away. "And what of the Vondod?"

"As I told you, they are gone."

"Gone? Not dead?" Her tone was biting.

"Had they killed you, I would have reciprocated. But I still feel responsible in a way. I made them what they are."

"Because they wanted you to!"

Dagsbrún sighed. "True, but we all must be responsible for what our instincts make us do."

Anda began to pace the floor. Her temper flaring. "And what do your instincts tell you to do with me?"

He stared at her. "What do my instincts tell me to do?"

"You can kill, fly, and heal. But you could not be there to stop your wraiths. You swept in at the opportune moment and whisked me back to my room and then watched me as I slept?"

Dagsbrún was taken aback by her words. "Anda, I am sorry. I am not invulnerable. Another vampire abused their power to accentuate my weakness. And yes, I did bring you back to your room. I carried you slowly back to your room and set you in your bed. And then I sat in the chair all night."

"Why?"

Dagsbrún's shoulders slumped. "Because… I do not know why. I was concerned for you."

"Concerned for me?" She raised her fists and beat them against his chest. "Your property? Your prisoner?"

He was trying incredibly hard not to lose his temper. He gripped her wrists and firmly lowered her arms. "Not my property. Not my prisoner. My equal."

She would not let herself be bested by his words. "Me? A halfling? A half-blood?"

He held her firmly. "Half-elf. Half-powerful elf.

She could feel herself surrendering, but she fought back. "Compared to a half-elf, half-vampire, I am nothing."

His face was inches from hers. "You are everything."

Anda fell silent. She had no more words. His eyes pulled her in, and she was lost.

He pulled her closer, their bodies melting into one another. "Anda, I…"

He was interrupted by a loud knock at her door. They both turned as Gammel and Vandre fell into the room. Gammel's eyes darted around the room as though he were looking for something or someone that was not there.

Anda pulled away from Dagsbrún. "Out of all of you, I would have thought that you would possess the best manners, Gammel. It appears I was wrong."

Gammel let out a relieved sigh. "Vandre found and told me everything. Where are those harpies?"

Dagsbrún did not hide his annoyance. "Gone, Gammel. As you have wished for years. They tried to kill Anda last night, and I banished them."

"I saw them jump out the window," Vandre replied, still incredibly pale. "I thought it was a dream. Good riddance!"

"Yes, yes," Dagsbrún snapped. "You all despised them, as did I. But let us remember all our flaws. None of us are perfect. Their imperfections were simply more prevalent."

"Good riddance indeed!" Gammel crossed to Anda. "But there are larger demons you must now face. The Vale is crumbling. Elf and Vampire are destroying themselves and their world. You must leave. Now!"

"Now?" Anda looked at Dagsbrún and then back at Gammel.

"She has been enough, Gammel. Can it not wait?" Dagsbrún knew without an answer that there was no waiting.

Vandre stepped forward, pulling his tunic sleeves down over the marks on his arms. "I know that I am nothing compared to the two of you, but I would gladly follow and be of whatever I can be."

Anda smiled. "But this is not your fight."

"If you do not succeed in the Vale, then it will be my fight."

Anda had no response to Vandre's words. She managed a small smile and enveloped Vandre in a tender embrace.

Gammel looked hopeful. "Does this mean you will go?

Anda nodded. "I will go."

With, and most certainly by magic, Anda was dressed and standing in the courtyard in less than an hour. Gammel had produced breeches, a breastplate molded to her form, sword, and food to last at least a month. Anda had learned not to ask where things came from, only that they would appear when needed.

When she had entered the courtyard, Droime had appeared as if he had been summoned. Vandre brought a saddle from the stable but had been unsure as to how to put it on a kelpie. Dagsbrún had taken the saddle and gingerly placed it on Droime's back. The kelpie snorted and pawed the ground, but otherwise kept still.

Once he was saddled, Anda climbed on his back. She could feel his weight move and shift under her thighs, but he was much calmer than the kelpie she had met on their last two encounters. She ran her hand down his neck and through his mane, trying to deepen their connection. She knew he would need his endurance and protection.

As she thought of protection, her gaze wandered to Dagsbrún. He had dawned a cloak and strapped a sword to his side, but his hair still hung wild, and he had not bothered to don a shirt. He handed a saddlebag to Vandre, who took it and threw it over his shoulder. Across his other shoulder, Vandre shouldered a long bow and a quiver of arrows. Anda wondered what arrows could do against the foes they were bound to face.

The small party made their way out of the courtyard and to the forest. They were quiet, each lost in their own thoughts. The burden of their duty and destiny lay upon each of their shoulders. Gammel led the way, and it seemed to Anda that he somehow seemed older than he had that morning. He would not join them; he had told her. His presence would be too noticeable and too strongly felt by the elves,

They reached the archway and stopped. Anda dismounted, and gently led Droime up the steps. Vandre and Dagsbrún followed behind her. The four of them turned to look back at Gammel. He reached inside his cloak and pulled a piece of what appeared to be quartz from its folds. He held it out to Anda.

"It is called *Asestein,*" he said. "If you ever need aid, you have only to use it and I will come."

Anda smiled. "I thought you wanted us to be inconspicuous."

Gammel chuckled. "If you have need of me, you will no longer be inconspicuous."

Anda reached out and tenderly touched the wizened elf's face. "I will always have need of you, Gammel. You have taught me more in a few weeks, than the world taught me in a lifetime."

He gripped her hand firmly and then gently pulled it back. "Now, go."

Anda stepped back and turned toward the archway. She heard Gammel strike the ground with his staff and felt a rush wind through the trees, but she could not bear to look back at the elf, for fear her heart would make her change her mind.

"Åpne for meg! Åpne for oss! Matte vi krysse inn i din verden, for vi var av ditt blod![4]"

---

[4] Translates to: "Open unto me. Open unto us. May we cross into your world, for we are of your blood" in Gaelic.

Gammel's voice echoed through the trees and deep into the earth, causing the roots of the forest to reverberate. Just as it had with Dagsbrún, the space between the columns shifted and changed to reveal a meadow of tall grasses and tiny white flowers.

Dagsbrún approached the threshold of the space between the turn worlds and looked over his shoulder. He was nearly blinded by the bright light pouring from Gammel's staff. He did not know if the old man could see him, and so shouted, "*Jeg er din*[5]!"

From beyond the blinding light, he heard Gammel reply, "Du er min[6]*!"*

Dagsbrún smiled and turned toward the Vale. Putting his hand out in front of him, he crossed over into the world he was born from, followed close behind by Vandre.

Anda urged Droime through and paused before crossing. I am terrified, Gammel, she called out with her mind.

We are creatures of fear, he replied. We must become more than what our fear makes us. Go now, Halfling.

Anda turned and looked at Gammel, tears filling her eyes. He smiled and raised his staff over his head.

"Gammel, I can't!"

"Go!" he shouted. "Become what we believe you to be!"

He smashed his staff into the ground, the force hurling Anda through the archway.

The trees quieted, the roots settled, and the wind silenced. Gammel was left standing in the middle of the clearing, alone for the first time in centuries.

---

[5] *Jeg er din* means "I am yours" in Danish.
[6] *Du er min* means "You are mine" in Danish.

Chapter 14

Her body was pulled through what felt like thick water, fluid but oppressive. She instinctively held her breath, though she was unsure how that would possibly save her from drowning in a vortex of space. Just when she thought she would suffocate, her hand felt fresh air. She tumbled through the opening into another world with the grace of a goat, landing face down in the dirt.

She felt the soft nuzzle of Droime's nose in her neck. Groaning, she rolled over, spitting out dirt as she did so. "Does it always feel like that?"

Dagsbrún reached out his hand. "I would not know. The last time I went through I was an infant."

She took his hand and rose to her feet. "You have never been back?" He shook his hand. "And we are supposed to somehow end certain destruction for a world we have never been to except you, in a swaddling blanket."

"We have Gammel's maps. What could go wrong?"

Vandre strode between them. "Bloodsucking vampires. Magic-wielding elves. Creatures and landscapes that most certainly welcome outsiders. And an impending war. What could go wrong indeed?"

They followed him. "Well, thank you very much," Anda shouted. " I was not thinking about the creatures and landscapes until you said something!"

Dagsbrún pulled a folded map from his knapsack. Opening it up, he traced his finger along a faded line. "We walk East. Gammel said to go to the Elvish capital, Calina. He believes the elves might be more willing to listen than the vampires."

"Well, they are more biologically represented in this group," Vandre pointed out.

"True," Anda agreed. "But we also significantly represent the human race. Which one will they recognize?"

Dagsbrún shook his head. "I do not know, but we must try. It will take two days to reach Calina."

"And that is without any misadventure between here and there," Anda shifted her sword. "I cannot imagine we will go unmatched if the elves are at war."

"That is why we stick to the mountain range and come into the city through the forest. There will be elves in the forest, but they do not enjoy the cold and so will be less likely to be in the mountains."

"So, we are going the most difficult route?" Vandre groaned.

Anda slapped the back of his head. "Would you rather be stabbed or bitten?"

"No," Vandre mumbled.

They traveled much farther than what the map seemed to say. The weather was almost as inconsistent as Dagsbrún's moods: one-minute glorious sunlight, the next terrifying thunderstorms with rain that was blinding. He wrestled with the two halves that made him. His elf half was drawn to Calina, but his vampire half pushed back with all its might. Each step was a struggle, and the journey for him was both a physical one and one within himself.

The trio made their way across the mountain range of Roin. The trail was uneven and treacherous, with sheer drops that offered only death on the jagged rocks below. Rarely was there shelter from the elements, save an occasional outcropping in the mountainside. Many nights Droime would lay down, and Vandre and Anda would sleep against him for warmth while Dagsbrún kept watch. He could not help but think it was strange that they had met no one on the road. Not a traveler nor a soldier. There had not been a single beast visible save the occasional crow or dragonfly.

After four days, they reached the end of the mountain trail and entered the forests of Gwyrdd. The sheltering trees were a welcome relief from the onslaught of wind and rain. Droime immediately seemed happier as there were no longer rocks pricking at his hooves. The pathway was dark but flat and even.

After a day of traveling in the forest, they could see Calina through the distant trees. From far off, it was nothing impressive, merely a plain stone wall rising above the trees. But Dagsbrún had painted a picture of vine-covered gardens, marble statues, and tranquil ponds. Where the vampire kingdom was dark and silent, Calina was shining and full of life.

"We will enter through the Shepherd's Gate," he had told Anda. "We will do our best to blend in with the travelers coming from the north. Hopefully, we will be overlooked."

"And if we're not?"

He smiled. "Then we will hope your charming personality will win them over."

Anda chuckled. "So, we are most certainly doomed."

His gaze softened. "You have your moments."

"Which moments?

"I am not sure. But you have been charming at times. Be like that."

She scoffed. "I am never charming. We may as well turn around now."

Droime entered her thoughts. *You are more than what you think yourself to be. You made me believe in you. Now, believe in yourself.*

Anda reached down and stroked his neck. "Thank you, friend," she said aloud.

"What did he say?" Vandre asked.

"That he has manners," she retorted.

They reached the wall at the end of the fifth day. It stretched out into the distance until it disappeared on the horizon. There was a road that ran through a small double-door gate, but other than that the trees grew up against the wall. The trio was relieved to see a steady stream of travelers entering the city.

"Why are there so many?" Anda asked.

"Vampires likely are laying waste to the villages."

"But why?" Vandre interjected.

"Vampires have no manners when it comes to war." He turned toward the crowd entering the gate. "These people have nothing left save for the hope that Calina will protect them."

"And if we fail, Calina fails?"

"The two are interchangeable. If the elves fail to be hospitable, they will play a part in our demise. If we fail to stop the war, then we will be to blame."

They waited for night to fall and then joined the throng flowing into the city. Pulling their hoods tightly over their faces, they merged into the middle of the crowds. They were shuffled back and forth with the rocking and jostling of the crowd. Everyone was so intent on passing through the gate that no one looked out for their neighbor. The sentries at the gate had lost control of ushering people into the city in an orderly fashion. Instead, they stood on either side of the gate with spears at the ready should there be any sort of commotion.

Dagsbrún had warned them to keep their eyes lowered and hoods pulled up over their faces, but Anda could not help but look about her. The city was situated amongst a series of hills-the gates, and armory at the bottom. From there, white cobbled streets ran through the market and town square up to the shops. From there, the road wound over a bridge that crossed a gentle waterfall to the townspeople's homes. They were made of stone, with rooms covered in thatch. Wooden doors and shutters were beautifully designed with flowing images of floral and animal wildlife. From these homes, the road cut through a small forest. Dagsbrún explained that this was the elves' sacred place—the forest of Naofa. Here, the elders met, and weddings were held. Here, elder elves taught the young ones to use their magic. After crossing another bridge, the forest gave way to a graveled road that led to the palace.

Suiochan Ard.

The high seat of the elves. The heart of their world. Here was their mecca, their pulse. Cut from ancient marble, the palace shone in effervescent brilliance. Like the city, it rose to the heavens in a series of angular levels. Statues of ancient founders of Calina lined the path to the main door that had been hewn out of wood and iron. This door was much more heavily guarded than the gate to enter the city, and the trio knew this would be where they needed to make themselves known.

"Let me do the talking," Dagsbrún whispered as approached the group of elfin soldiers. He kept his hood raised, but Anda saw him put his hand on the hilt of his sword. She reached for Droime's bridle and pulled him to stop.

"What do you think our chances are?" Vandre whispered.

"An incredibly small chance," she whispered back.

"Marvelous."

Dagsbrún stopped as the elfin guard moved to block the door. "Greetings, brothers! We seek an audience with Rioghail and the rest of the Eldern."

"What business is it that you have?" one of the guards asked.

"It is of the utmost urgency and secrecy," Dagsbrún replied.

"Unless you tell us, we cannot let you pass."

"As I said, it is urgent."

The guard took a step forward. "And as I said, we cannot let you pass. The Eldern's safety is our one and only duty."

Anda was done with the banter. She pushed past Dagsbrún and pulled her hood off her head, exposing her pointed ears and bright hair. "It is all very fine and well for you males to stand around challenging one another like beasts in the wild, but there are bigger problems that we must address!"

Dagsbrún gripped her shoulder. "Anda!"

She shrugged him off. "Look!" she pointed at her ears. "I am one of you, as is he. The boy is our servant. We were allowed to pass through the gate, so those guards approved. If Rioghail does not, you can throw us out."

The guard motioned to the other guards to step aside, never taking his eyes off Anda and Dagsbrún. "If Rioghail does not approve of what you have to say, then we will lock you away in the deepest dungeon with our dragon."

Dagsbrún chuckled. "Since when does the Eldern have a dragon?"

The guard did not laugh. "Since we stole the egg from the vampires and raised it as our own."

"Well, that makes things even more unsettling," Vander muttered.

Anda glared at him and then turned back to the guard. "That is completely fair. Let Rioghail decide."

The guard turned and walked to the door. He lifted the giant wooden beam and set it to one side. Lifting an iron latch, he and another guard pushed the door open. It swung inward with a loud groan, crashing into the wall with a thud that echoed down the hall. Without another word, they walked away.

Dagsbrún turned to Vandre. "Bring Droime."

"Inside?"

"He is a kelpie, not a stable horse! Bring him!"

He turned and brushed past Anda. She knew he was angry with her for speaking. She followed without another word, and Vandre brought up the rear with Droime.

This is not a wise decision, Droime told her.

It is the only choice we have, she replied.

There is evil in this place, he said.

She pulled her cloak close. *There is evil everywhere.*

The guards escorted them down a long, narrow hall, lit with torches in gilded scones and candles on ornate tables. The stone walls were bedecked with vibrant tapestries that depicted various scenes of elves.

"It is their history," Dagsbrún whispered to her.

"Yes, thank you," she retorted. "I can see that."

"They came from the darkness, and the ancient one called Dhia gave them light. He taught them about beauty and music and how to treasure and protect the world around them. They built vast civilizations, beautiful cities, and opulent palaces. The elves became wise but also vain."

Anda smiled. "I do not think their vanity is recorded in their history.

He nodded. "That is my own input. They considered themselves superior to other races—man and vampire alike. And while they still treasured the nature they were taught to nurture; they began to see others as the enemy."

"Arrogance will often do that."

"The Eldern was formed to try and instill the ideals of Dhia into the younger generations, but it is rumored that even that has been corrupted."

"By whom?

"No one knows, so secret are their meetings. It could be Rioghail, it could be his sister."

"His sister?"

"Bearla." A shadow passed over his face.

Anda saw it. "Why the change in expression?

He shrugged his shoulders. "It is nothing."

She would have pushed further, but they turned a corridor and approached another great door, this one laden in gold. The guard who had spoken with them motioned them to stop. He cracked open the door and stepped through to the other side.

"Wait here," he said and slammed the door shut.

"Do us all a favor," Dagsbrún whispered. "Do not talk in there."

"It seems that my talking was what got us this far in the first place," she retorted.

Dagsbrún sighed. "You may have a point."

She was surprised by his willingness to agree. "Well," she cleared her throat. "I would be more than happy to speak… should you lose your ability to do so."

He laughed. "Oh, believe me. I have more than enough to say to Rioghail."

The door swung open wide, and the guard reemerged. He motioned for them to enter. They stepped inside the door which led into a great hall. It was wide and silent with high vaulted ceilings graced with wooden arches. The floor was an intricate mosaic of colored geometric patterns. At the far end of the hall, the floor raised to a dais in a series of steps. On top of the dais sat a long table gilded in gold. And at the table sat six individuals.

The Eldern.

The guard hit his spear against the floor and shouted. "Kneel!"

The trio immediately did so, their knees hitting the floor and causing an echo to cascade backward out of the room.

They heard chairs scraping backward and footsteps approaching. They stopped directly in front of Anda. She peered out from clenched eyelids to see pointed golden boots nearly touching her knees. She turned her head ever so slightly to look upward and saw a face gazing down at her.

Rioghail.

Chapter 15

The room was uncomfortably silent. Anda could hear water dripping from the leaves outside the window. She was unsure as to who was supposed to act first. After waiting what seemed like hours, Anda moved to rise.

Dagsbrún gripped her arm. "Do not move," he hissed. "He is testing you."

A low rumble reverberated across the floor and rose up the walls, changing into the sound of bells tinkling. Anda raised her head and looked at her host. He had thrown his head back, and the musical sound was his laughter. The Eldern looked down at Anda and offered her his hand.

"Sizing you up, not testing," Rioghail pulled her up to her feet. "It is not every day a sprite such as yourself graces Suiochan Ard."

His eyes were piercing, penetrating. They were a deep, velvety amethyst color, set in a face that almost seemed as though it were made of stone, with perfectly chiseled cheekbones and nose. He was pale, but not the ghostly hue of Dagsbrún. There was a slight flush to his cheeks, perfectly matching his glistening lips. Anda found herself uncertain as to how to respond. She sensed immense power, but also a being that was common in nature. His eyes did not move from her face, nor did he let go of her hand. She could think of nothing articulate to say, and so she simply muttered,

"Thank you, Milord,"

"Rioghail, to someone as fair you," he replied. He gently touched her chin and raised it to meet her eyes. "Who might you be?"

"My name is Anda."

His smile widened. "Anda. A beautiful name. Tell me, Anda, from whence do you come?"

Dagsbrún rose to his feet and Rioghail's smile immediately vanished. He let go of Anda's arm and reached for his sword.

"Dagsbrún." Rioghail spoke his name as though he were sipping poison.

Dagsbrún gave a curt nod. "Rioghail. You have not changed much since the last time our paths crossed."

"I thought you had left our world," the Eldern replied.

"I have returned."

Rioghail raised an eyebrow. "A pity."

Anda knew they were getting nowhere. She stepped between them. "Please, Milord. We have information for the Eldern."

Rioghail seemed surprised. "News, fair one? What information could one so beautiful have that was of importance to those such as us?"

Anda was taken aback. "I am not just a fair face, Milord."

He smiled. "Indeed?"

"In fact, I do not consider myself fair at all."

Rioghail reached out and pushed a stray strand of hair away from her face. "Fair and witty," he murmured. "Tell me what you have to say, and we will see if you are also wise in doing so."

Anda looked at Dagsbrún. "He is far more equipped to tell you our purpose here."

Rioghail shook his head. "No, I want to hear it from you."

Anda could feel her anxiety growing. She was growing weary and wanted this to be over and done with. She looked passed Rioghail to the others sitting around the table. "We are weary,

Milord. We have traveled for many days with little rest. Might I address all the Eldern at once?"

He smiled. "Share with me, and I will relay your news."

Now he was rubbing her nerves. "Please, Milord. Our information is to be given to the Eldern in its entirety."

Rioghail was impressed. Perhaps he had underestimated this sprite who had crossed into his world. He stepped to the side and gestured to the table where the Eldern were seated. "Please, Lady Anda. We would hear what you have to say."

She felt both relief and renewed apprehension. She lowered her eyes and walked past him toward the Eldern. She knew what she needed to say, but the words were rolling around in her mind and she could not think how to put together a coherent sentence. She stared at her boots as she walked across the tiles, leaving dusty footprints on the spotless floor.

She reached the edge of the dais, her shoes touching the bottom step. Breathing deeply, she raised her eyes and looked at the Eldern. There were five of them sitting, four men and one woman. The men looked at her with bemusement, while the woman stared at her with judgment in her eyes. Anda was more unnerved by the one woman than the five men combined.

"Bearla."

Anda was relieved to feel Dagsbrún behind her, his breath cascading down her neck and back.

She turned her head to look at him. His eyes were reassuring, but his mouth was pursed in a tight, grim line.

He stepped closer. "Bearla, Rioghail's sister."

"She is trying to murder me with her eyes," Anda whispered.

"Out of all the Eldern, she is the one with the most venom." Dagsbrún looked up at the female Eldern. "And she does not have any affection for me."

Anda grounded. "How is it you have offended someone from a world you do not even live in?"

He smiled. "I did not always live in your world."

"You left here when you were an infant!"

"There might have been a time when I returned. When I was…"

"Intemperate? Rebellious?"

He sighed. "Something along those lines."

Anda's temper flared. She turned back to the Eldern, willing herself to be calm.

Rioghail climbed the steps to this chair and sat down. "Fellow Eldern, this is Lady Anda. She has come with news most urgent."

The Eldern to the right of Rioghail leaned forward. "Where to you hail from, Lady Anda?"

She knew there was no retreating now.

"My lords, and lady, I have come from the world beyond the Vale, with news bearing the fate of both our worlds."

There was a murmur amongst them. The same Eldern gripped the table. "You come from the world beyond the Vale? You are, human?"

"I am…"

The murmur turned to a road. A ruddy-haired elder jumped to his feet. "Throw them out! Throw them back through the portal!"

Rioghail raised his hand. "Let her speak."

She squared her shoulders. "I am half human. My mother was an elf from this world." The table grew quiet, and so she continued. "My mother crosse the Vale in a storm, and my father saved her. I was born with her gift, though I did not know it was such a thing until I was driven from my village. I fled for my life, and the safety of my father, sister, and her family. I found myself in wild woods, and it was there that the boy, Vandre found me."

The Eldern whispered amongst themselves and Rioghail leaned forward, resting his elbows on the table. "Dear one, we appreciate your most fascinating biography, but this is hardly fodder that is of any importance to us."

She cleared her throat. "The boy took me to his home, The Castle Skog. Here I met Dagsbrún, the half-elf, and Gammel, the great elfin teacher."

"It may interest the Eldern to know the large oaf standing behind the half-elf is none other than the great Dagsbrún himself," Rioghail interjected.

The murmur returned. Bearla leaned forward, her eyes widening. "Dagsbrún?" she whispered. "Is it truly you?"

Dagsbrún removed his hood and the room erupted. "I am he."

Rioghail raised his hand once more. His face was covered in smugness. "Now that we have all been properly introduced, save for the wild horse in the back, do continue, Anda."

Anda sighed. "Gammel taught me that my gifts were power. He showed me how to harness and control it. The wild horse that you mention is a kelpie. For my final task in mastering my power, I was ordered to call my Familiar. This kelpie, known as Droime, was who appeared."

"A kelpie is your Familiar?" the Eldern to Rioghail's right asked.

She nodded. "We have a bond that cannot be broken and speak to each other with our thoughts."

"This is all very enchanting," Bearla replied. "But it is fodder for a story told to a child."

Anda felt her temper rising to the surface. "The purpose in Gammel teaching and guiding me was because he has seen our fate. The fate of both our worlds." The Eldern grew silent. "He has seen our ruin, the complete destruction of the elf, the vampire, and the humans if there is no reconciliation."

"You want us to call off the war?" the ruddy-headed elder bellowed. "Retreat from the vampires, and let them run rampant with their blood thirst?"

Anda shook her head. "Find a way to make peace. The fighting, the endless bickering has caused the delicate web, the Gréasáin, we all walk upon to begin to break."

"Nonsense," Bearla replied. "We have been at war with the vampires since the First Dawn. Why now?"

This time it was Dagsbrún who replied. "Because now there is an answer. A way to recompense all the hatred."

Bearla arched an eyebrow. "Really? And I suppose you think you are the savior?"

He shook his head. "Not myself." He put his hand firmly on Anda's shoulder. "Her."

Bearla's face grew dark with rage. "Impossible! She is a halfblood! A blemish on the elvish race!"

Rioghail's chuckled. "Quiet, sister. Lest your jealousy betray you." He turned back to Anda. "If what Dagsbrún says is true, then just exactly what do you propose to do about it?" Anda blinked. She was at a loss as to how to respond. She bit her lip and looked down. Rioghail rose from his chair and walked around the table and down the steps. He lifted her chin once more. "Now, now. Do not lose your voice now. How do you plan to stop the downfall of two worlds?"

Anda knew he was mocking her. "I do not know, Milord."

He clicked his tongue. "Oh, you do not know? Well, then, exactly why are we supposed to listen to any more of this nonsense?"

"It is not nonsense!" she clasped her hands tightly. "I cannot explain it. Gammel sees something in me that I must confess I do not even see. I know I possess my mother's gifts; I have used them. But as to how I am to bring peace, I do not know."

"Wait!" Bearla held up her hand. She leaned intently across the table, her eyes scrutinizing Anda. "She *does* know. I can see her thoughts. She knows how to bring peace but is keeping it secret!"

"That is not true!" Anda shouted.

Rioghail's eyes narrowed. "Bearla is most adept at reading thoughts. So, let us cease all the tiresome bantering. What is your secret? How will you restore balance?"

Anda looked over her shoulder at Dagsbrún and then back at Rioghail. "With…"

Rioghail gripped her arm. "Yes?"

The silence was shattering. Rioghail let go of her arm and stepped back. "I see. Forbindelse. A connection that is most divine. And just whom do you need to connect with?"

She wished she could see Dagsbrún face. She was unsure as to whether she should reveal what Gammel had said. Did it even truly matter? She looked up at Rioghail. He smiled, encouraging her with his eyes. His voice had been harsh, but there was something enticing about those eyes. She bit her lip absent-mindedly and replied,

"I do not know." She heard Dagsbrún inhale sharply behind her. Perhaps she had said the wrong thing.

Rioghail's smile widened. "Well then," he replied. "We shall have to remedy that."

"Why should we help them?" Bearla shouted.

Rioghail ignored her. "Tonight, we shall host our guests and tomorrow we shall go to the Naofa woods and seek our answers there." He motioned to the guards. "Find rooms for our guests." Turning back to Anda he said, "We will find your answers, my lady. Tomorrow will go to the forest and consult the learned elves there. Tonight, I would be honored if you would dine at my table."

She was not sure if she should be honored or alarmed. She bowed her head and replied, "As you wish, my lord." She turned to follow the guards.

Dagsbrún grabbed her arm. "Just what are you playing at? Rioghail cannot be trusted. And now we are eating at his table? We are likely to be poisoned!"

She pried his fingers off her arm. "He will not harm us. He needs answers. Do you best to not act like a beast." She turned and followed the guard out the door, Vandre and Droime followed behind her.

"I am not the beast here," Dagsbrún grumbled and followed after them.

The Eldern dispersed and went their separate ways. Only Rioghail and Bearla remained. He returned to his seat and looked at his sister with a smug look.

She sneered at him. "Oh, do not look so smug! You are treading dangerously close to doom, brother."

He rested his arms on his chair. "I am not smug. I am quite sure you and I are about to have the most extraordinary gratification. Both of us getting a little back from what that half-breed took from us."

"You seemed got taken with that half-breed."

He chuckled. "Not that one, the other one. I know a way for you to get the revenge you always wanted."

It was Bearla's turn to laugh. "Do tell."

He leaned towards her, his face curling in malice. "We must break the *Forbindelse*."

Chapter 16

The guards took the Anda and Dagsbrún to rooms in the western part of the palace. Anda had asked Vandre to stay with Droime who refused to stay in the stables, and so they retreated to a small clearing near the woods.

Droime had protested leaving Anda. *You are in grave danger here,* nickered softly.

I know, she had replied. *But sadly, a kelpie in my room would be absurd to the elves.*

You have only to think, and I will be by your side.

She had stroked his mane tenderly. Anda had grown quite fond of the magical horse that had once tried to drown her. She watched Vandre and Droime leave the palace filled with an overwhelming sense of doubt. Dagsbrún believed her to have made the wrong decision, though what the right decision was, she did not know. Rioghail was arrogant but also alluring. She could not tell if he mocked her because he was intrigued by her, or because he thought her inferior in all aspects. As for his sister, she was certain Bearla wanted her dead.

Dagsbrún had entered his room and slammed the door shut. Anda turned and resignedly went to her room, shutting the door with more decorum than him. Turning the lock, she looked around. There was already a fire roaring in the fireplace. On the bed, someone had laid a gown out for her. Lifting it up, she determined that this place was full of simple magic. Not the magic that took learning, but that which came with the snap of one's fingers. Still, she wondered how a fire had been built and a dress and been procured in a matter of minutes.

The sun cast an array of reddish beams and shadows and it began to sink beneath the horizon. She hurriedly removed her traveling clothes and laced herself into it. She let her hair fall loose about her shoulders, unsure as to how to fashion it. She had no shoes but her filthy boots and so resigned to going barefoot.

There was a knock at the door. She reached for her sword and then crossed the room to open it. Dagsbrún stood there, leaning against the wall. His eyes widened at the sight of her in the gown. Seeing her, he stood upright and awkwardly brushed his breeches.

She smirked. "Did you wish to come in or were you going to take up space in the hall?"

His eyes narrowed. "I came to check on you."

"Check on me?" She scoffed. "I am not a foaling mare. I can take care of myself."

He pushed past her into her room. "Do you have the slightest idea of the viper's nest you have created?"

Her temper boiled. "No, I do not have the slightest idea. And this is because you have kept everything from me. It is plain as the sun setting that there is something between you and Bearla, and possible even Rioghail. We are playing with millions of lives, and yet you still do not trust me enough to tell me everything!"

Dagsbrún paced the room like a caged animal. He turned and looked outside the window and then back at her. "When I was younger, I visited Calina. I was allowed because I was half-elf. The villagers and the Eldern treated me like a monster, but one that had lost its teeth and claws."

Anda smiled wryly. "And had you?"

"Of course not. I believe they wanted to gawk, to treat me like an untrained pet." He paused. "All but one."

Anda grimaced. "Bearla."

He sighed. "Again, I was young and completely uncentered. Bearla seemed to admire me."

"Admire you?"

"We would walk in the forest and spend hours talking by the fire. I felt appreciated and accepted. As though finally someone saw me as a whole being, not a monster with dual personalities."

Anda sighed, "But she was not what she seemed?"

He shook his head. "One night she came to my room. I was old enough to know what she wanted, but I was afraid to touch her. I did not know if my instinct, my blood thirst would take over. She begged me to embrace her, but I refused."

"I assume Bearla is not used to being denied what she wants."

"She went to Rioghail and told him I had disgraced her. He was enraged. But like with everything, Rioghail tried to manipulate the situation for his gain. He believed that if his sister were married to a vampire, at least a half-vampire, his position would be strengthened. He ordered me to wed his sister."

"And you refused."

He nodded. "Refused and retreated. Completely. I flew back to Gammel. But Bearla was disgraced. To the elves, she was permanently tainted for having interacted with a vampire. She nearly lost her place amongst the Eldern. Rioghail lost control of the city for a time. No one trusted the brother and sister who had entertained a vampire."

Anda pursed her lips. "Still, he seems to be flourishing."

Dagsbrún shrugged. "It is his greatest gift. He makes people see what he wants."

"Perhaps he is not as flawed as he seems."

His face grew dark. "Has he cast his spell on you too?

She shook her head. "Rioghail has only been gracious. His mannerisms are dignified."

The cloud across his face grew darker. "Yes, and he is quite wonderful to gaze upon."

Anda blushed. "It is not that in the least."

"Oh, is it not?" he scoffed.

"No!" Before she could take another breath, Dagsbrún had gripped her arms and pinned her against the wall. His eyes blazed with an intensity that made her want to scream, but oxygen would not enter her lungs. His lips parted to reveal his teeth. She met his gaze and whispered the same reply again. "No."

His grip softened ever so slightly. "You think him a god, and I, a beast."

She bit her lip. "No."

"Perhaps I am. But then, perhaps he is too."

Tears were beginning to fill her eyes. "Dagsbrún, I am not comparing you to him. I barely know Rioghail."

He would not move. "And yet, you think him gracious and dignified."

"I only meant…"

He slammed his hand against the wall. "I know what you meant!" he inhaled sharply. "Anda, do you have any inclination as to the torment you instill in me? Half of me wants to destroy you." He placed his finger on the curve of her neck and felt her pulse pounding. "I want to sink my teeth into the place between your collar and your jawline." His teeth came to rest on the surface of her skin, and she quivered. He sighed and pulled back ever so slightly. "But the other half of me wants nothing more than to be your refuge. And so help me, if anyone were to harm you…"

"You'd what?" she murmured. "Dig your teeth into them instead? Because they took what you think is yours?"

His eyes softened. "You belong to me no more than Droime belongs to you. I told you this that morning at Castle Skog. You are not my possession, nor my inferior. You are my equal." He ran his finger along her collarbone. "But that does not mean I do not wish to belong to you."

Anda felt the flush in her cheeks deepen, and her legs grow weak. She turned her chin up slightly. "Then I suggest you act upon that desire."

He leaned closer. "I cannot."

"You WILL not."

He moved his finger to the curvature of her ear and traced its line to the back of her neck. "I cannot. You need to tell me."

She snickered. "That is a bit archaic."

Dagsbrún spread his hand along her neck and pulled close once more. "Part of the vampire code." He feared he could crush her, so firm was his grip. "Say it."

Anda was drowning in his eyes, his voice, his breath. "I…"

A knock at the door broke the spell being woven. Dagsbrún grunted and slammed his hand once more into the wall. Anda turned her head toward the door.

"Would you mind getting that?" she asked.

Without taking his eyes off her face, he reached his hand out, lifted the latch, and pulled open the door.

Rioghail.

He stood there with a bemused look on his face, leaning against the corridor wall with an arrogance that immediately vexed Dagsbrún.

"Did you need something?" he growled.

Rioghail smiled. "I certainly hope I am not interrupting."

Anda ducked under Dagsbrún's arm and offered her hand to Rioghail. "Not in the least." She heard Dagsbrún growl behind her. "We were just making ready to dine with you."

Rioghail examined her for a moment before taking her hand, kissing it, and linking it to his. "Delightful. I came to escort you to dinner."

"We would have been able to find it without help," Dagsbrún grumbled.

Rioghail laughed as he pulled Anda into the corridor. "Will you be joining us, Dagsbrún? I should think our food is not quite the fare you are used to."

Dagsbrún followed behind them. "I will make due."

Rioghail led them down the long corridor to a winding spiral staircase. It wove its way down through the palace to the main floor. Crossing through yet another corridor, Rioghail led them into a great hall, like the one where the Eldern had sat. This one held several long wooden tables bedecked with rich and vibrant food and golden pitchers of wine. Above this room was a large mezzanine, with stone railings graced with colorful pendants. Here sat half a dozen musicians playing music. Several elves had already begun to eat, but they all turned to acknowledge Rioghail when they entered the room.

"They are wondering who you are," Rioghail whispered.

"I am sure they are forming all sorts of colorful opinions," she replied.

At the far end of the hall stood a great stone table that ran perpendicular to the others. Here the Eldern now stood, watching them approach. Anda knew they were waiting to personally meet her. Their eyes pierced through her soul, and she knew they were searching out every weakness, every flaw.

As they approached the Eldern table, Dagsbrún pulled away and found a place at the end of one of the tables. Anda sensed his departure and became even more uncomfortable. She gripped Rioghail's arm.

He chuckled and patted her hand, "Easy. They do not bite. At least no harder than your vampire." He led her to the first Eldern. It was the ruddy-haired elf from earlier. "This is Lasair."

Lasair bowed looked down at Anda over a perfectly pointed nose and nodded slightly. "Milady."

Anda bowed. "Milord."

Rioghail took her down the line as each passed silent judgment. There was Glorard, Airgid, Taidhleoir. Each looked at her with distrust and disdain. Finally, they came to Bearla. She was dressed in a sleeveless tunic made of a fabric threaded in silver. Her hair was plaited and piled high on her head, and she wore a circle of silver leaves around her forehead.

"And this is my sister."

Anda bowed. "Bearla."

Bearla nodded curtly. "Half-breed."

"Now Bearla," Rioghail gently tapped her shoulder. "She is our guest."

Bearla took a sip of her wine and turned to walk away. "Your guest. She is just a nuisance to me."

Anda tried to bite her tongue. But Bearla's smug look of disdain was too much. "Was Dagsbrún a nuisance to you?"

Bearla whirled back around. "You know nothing!"

Anda knew she was playing with fire. "I know people like you. People who think they are superior to everyone. You regard others as objects."

Bearla smirked. "Playthings."

"Dagsbrún would not give in to your play."

Bearla set her cup down on a table and crossed to Anda. She glared at her with piercing eyes. "There is always time for a second try."

Anda laughed. "I think you have had your chance."

Bearla leaned closer and whispered in Anda's ear. "You forget half-breed, I read thoughts. Yours... and his."

Anda felt her throat constrict. "I do not know what you speak of."

Bearla chuckled in her ear. "Oh, but I think you do."

Anda turned and looked at Dagsbrún. Her heart sank as she saw that his eyes were not on her, but on Bearla... He sensed her gaze and instantly shifted his gaze. But he saw the anger in her eyes and knew he had been caught.

Bearla's laughter grew louder. "See? His eyes are not for you."

"That is enough, Bearla." Rioghail pushed his sister away. He put his arm around Anda's waist. "Come, Anda." He pulled her to two seats at the end of the Eldern table. Pulling one away from the table, he offered it to her. She sat down and he pulled two glasses of wine off a tray as a steward passed by. "You must forgive my sister," he said, sitting down next to her.

Anda looked down at her reflection in the wine before draining her cup dry. "Must I forgive her?"

He laughed. "No, I suppose not." He poured her another glass from the pitcher on the table. "But I think it would be beneath you to hold a grudge."

It was Anda's turn to laugh. "You clearly do not know me."

"No, but I should like to." He reached out and gently turned Anda's hand over so that her palm was facing upward. Taking a finger, he ran it lightly along her wrist. "I should like to know everything about you."

Anda's head was light and her face warm. She knew it was the wine. She turned and looked for Dagsbrún, but he had left his place at the table. Looking over the crowd, she spotted him. He had joined the throng of dancers with Bearla. Her arms were draped across his shoulders as her hips swayed to the rhythm of the music. Anda could hear her lilting laughter above the music, and it grated against her heart.

"Lady Anda?"

Her attention was pulled away from the dancers back to Rioghail, his hand now loosely wrapped around her wrist.

She pulled away and smiled. "Please do not call me 'lady.' I am many things, but that is one thing I am not."

His eyes softened and he reached up to touch her cheek. "Is that so?"

She looked back towards Dagsbrún, whose eyes were fastened on Bearla. Anda's head was pounding. She shook it deftly. "No," she replied. "A lady is one thing I will never be."

Rioghail gently gripped her chin and turned her face back towards him. "Perhaps breeding and pedigrees are overvalued. You most certainly have other... merits."

She chuckled. "I could not tell you what they were. I was born in a small cottage with wolves howling at our door. I was exiled from my family and home because I could not control the powers my mother left me with. In fleeing, I became a prisoner at Castle Skog, discovered I was doomed to save all living things, and now I am here." She slammed her hand down on the table. "I am sitting at this table at a complete loss as to what I am supposed to do next."

Rioghail eyes changed ever so slightly. His charming smile shifted into a slight grin. He stood to his feet and offered his hand to Anda. "Come. I wish to show you something."

A small corner of Anda's mind told her not to go. But the voice was so distant, it was barely a whisper. She was tired of listening to her mind. Rising to her feet, she took his hand and followed him, Bearla's laughter followed her like the haunting of a thousand evil spirits.

Dagsbrún watched Anda leave with Rioghail from across the room. Rage filled him and for a split second, he envisioned himself laying waste to the hall, killing every one of the elves as they laughed and gorged themselves in their feasting. Where was Rioghail taking her? What was he concocting in that flaxen head of his?

Without realizing it, he gripped Bearla tighter, pulling her towards him. She laughed and responded by gripping his waist with one hand and placing her other hand on the back of his head. She forced him to look away from Anda and back at her.

"Just what is it that is tumbling around in that dark mind of yours?"

His eyes flashed. He could feel her trying to read his thoughts and reached up to remove her hand from his head. "You know you cannot pry my thoughts out, Bearla. You tried that once before."

She shrugged. "I thought perhaps you might have grown soft."

Dagsbrún pulled her close, flashing his teeth. "Not a century ago, not now. And never, ever for you."

Bearla was unwavering. "Pity. That will not help your precious halfling." She pushed away from him and made her way through the sea of feasters.

His temper soared. He tried to follow her, but the elvish dancers pushed back. He could no longer see her in the throng. What did she mean about Anda? What was she planning to do?

Come to me, and you will find out.

Dagsbrún froze. Bearla had found a way into his mind. She would dig and prod until she found the darkest corners and then she would use his secrets to destroy him… and Anda.

"Where are you?" he growled.

Come and find me.

Chapter 17

Anda followed Rioghail through a small side door, blissfully aware that her anger had dulled to a small, throbbing ache. She was wounded by Dagsbrún's seemingly blatant abandonment, but she had grown numb with wine.

He led her up a narrow set of stone steps to a great room atop a tower. The room was sparsely furnished and lined with balconies that looked out at the village, the forest, and across the land to the mountains.

As he entered the room, he dropped her hand and crossed to the balcony facing west. "The sky is on fire tonight."

She stood in the middle of the room, unsure as to what she should do or say. Crossing the room, she leaned against the balcony and breathed deeply. "I suppose a fiery sky is appropriate, considering the world is about to be aflame."

"You are the fire."

She looked sideways at Rioghail. "Pardon me?"

"You think you are nothing because you come from nowhere. But as I said, you possess other qualities. When the sun sets it scatters light, setting the sky ablaze with reds, oranges, and purples. It literally changes the direction of the light. It upsets what is normal throughout the normal course of a day." He turned to look at Anda. "You are the Firestarter. You were run out of your village because of it. Your flame will create an unstoppable inferno that will either ignite this world in inspiration or drown it in ash." He reached out and sank his fingers into her hair. "Either way, you have set me on fire."

The quiet voice in the corner of her mind grew slightly louder, warning her to flee. She shook her head and pulled away. "Then you best be careful, lest I drown you in ash."

He gripped her hand and pulled it to his chest. "Then set me aflame." He raised her hand to his lips and pressed his lips to her palm.

"Milord," she whispered.

"Rioghail. My name is Rioghail."

"*Lord* Rioghail."

He gripped her waist tightly. "Stay here. With me."

Her mind was a whirlwind. Rioghail had shifted from adversary to host to breaching every parameter she had built up around herself. There was no denying that he was striking, and his words were honeyed and sweet—a far cry from any conversation she had ever had with Dagsbrún.

But the voice inside her head was now screaming. Telling her to run. She pushed against his chest. "You flatter me. And in another time, perhaps…"

Her words were not to his liking. He pulled her back against him and then pushed her against the stone wall. "Enough talking. I am not unused to being denied what I want."

She laughed deliriously. "You were right. Breeding and pedigrees are overrated."

He gripped her face and squeezed. "And something you do not possess, halfling."

"How quickly your tune has changed, Milord. It was your sister who did the name-calling earlier."

"My sister?" he chuckled. "Oh, my sister. I wonder how she is faring with your vampire?" Anda's eyes widened. "You are surprised?" He laughed again. "Having met my sister did you think she was going to leave Dagsbrún alone? Bearla never forgets being slighted."

Anda groaned. "What is it you want? Revenge?

He leaned closer. "I want control. Bearla wants revenge."

She strained against him. "There is nothing for you to control."

He pushed her back. "I control you, I control the fate of this world. And yours."

Anda felt her mind caving in on itself. "But that has nothing to do with Dagsbrún."

His name on her lips enraged him. "It has everything to do with Dagsbrún!" He slammed his hand into the wall inches from her face. "You each are a half of a whole. You are less without the other. But that is because somewhere, deep down, you want to trust him. You want to need him."

"Never," she replied through gritted teeth.

"But it is true." his lips touched her chin. "How else do you explain forbindelse?"

Anda pushed against him. "There is no forbindelse between us!"

Her protests only encouraged him. "If there is nothing, then I should think I would be a worthy substitution." He leaned in and whispered in her ear, "Much like Bearla considers herself to be for you."

With all her might she pushed against Rioghail and looked him squarely in the face. "You are no substitution. For anything."

Rioghail wrenched her arm behind her back. "Even now, Bearla is convincing Dagsbrún how she is superior to you in every way. He will succumb to her whims. They always do. And then, forbindelse will be broken. Make it with me, and with your magic, we can rule the world."

Anda looked at the lust in his eyes and realized it was not for her, it was for power. She lifted her face up to his and replied, "Never." She twisted her arm free and darted away.

"Anda!"

"You are no better than the villagers who came after me with torches and pitchforks! You see something beyond your control, and you want to suppress, destroy it, and bend it to your will! You hold yourself in such high esteem, and yet you need a peasant to give you power."

"You are nothing without someone to harness your magic!"

"I need no one to harness anything!"

Rioghail laughed. "You need your vampire!"

Anda stamped her foot. "I need no one!" She stepped toward him. "And for all your railing against Dagsbrún, he has not once treated me in the manner you have!"

Rioghail's maniacal laughter did not stop. "If that is what you think, go to him. Go find him in Bearla's arms and see what your thoughts on him are then!"

Anda took a step towards the door. "He would not betray me."

"He would! He already has!"

Fighting against the terrifying urge to believe him, she turned towards the door and ran down the staircase. Rioghail's laughter rang in her ears.

Dagsbrún followed his heightened senses through a labyrinth of long, narrow corridors. They were silent, save for his own footsteps, and completely abandoned. He guessed the entirety of the palace was at the feast being held in Anda's honor, and she was not even there.

She was with Rioghail.

He clenched his fists. What was she thinking? Where was the good sense that Gammel had seen in her? Leaving with Rioghail was, in his opinion, only to spite him. But he could not understand what precisely he had done. He knew he was uncouth and had little in the way of mannerisms, but he had inadvertently been deemed Anda's protector. And as such, it was his duty to ensure her safety.

And he cared for her. Deeply.

There, he admitted it to himself. He cared for the half-human, half-elf. The spritely upstart who had appeared at his home and turned his world into total chaos, leaving him constantly at war with himself. He wanted to destroy her with his teeth and envelop her in his wings.

He had tried to tell her. First at Castle Skog after he had banished the Vondod, and then in her room before Rioghail interrupted them. He would have thought he had been transparent with his feelings, but she had absconded with the elf.

And now, he was following Bearla. Why? Was he so conflicted that perhaps he only half wanted Anda? He knew the elvish princess wanted to destroy him, and yet, he could not resist her voice.

Come to me.

His thoughts were drowned out by her voice. It wove through the columns and rafters like a thick fog. It consumed his being in its haunting tone, pulling him ever closer to her. He climbed a stairwell that led to another corridor.

Come.

The voice was louder and closer. He could feel her presence lingering nearby. He ran his hand along the smooth wall, trying to find her. A door creaked open, and her fragrance floated to his nostrils. He closed his eyes and inhaled deeply. Pushing the door farther open, he stepped into the room.

She was there, shining in the last rays of sunlight. Her skin radiated its beams as though her body was consumed with it. She danced to some silent tune, her arms twisting above her head, and her head and hips swayed to the invisible tune.

He knew she was aware of his presence. He sensed her heartbeat quicken as he approached, but she did not cease her dancing. The shoulder of her gown slipped down her arm, and she turned it towards him. He knew she was waiting to strike like a viper, but he would not play into her trap. He circled around her, stalking his own prey. Moving behind her, reached out and grabbed her.

"I should kill you here and now," he growled, wrapping his hand around her throat.

She chuckled. "But you will not."

He squeezed harder. "Why should I let you live?"

Bearla reached up and caressed his arm. "Because, you beast, if you kill me, Rioghail will kill Anda." She pulled his hand away from her throat and drifted across the room to sit in front of the fire. She turned her head back toward Dagsbrún and laughed once more. "Come now, beast. She is nothing to you. Come sit by the fire."

"She is everything to me," he hissed.

"Is she now?" This time, her laughter was shrill. "It is most amusing then that you followed me to my quarters while she is with my brother."

He stepped towards her. "I am sure that neither Anda nor I are in positions that are pleasurable."

Bearla held out her hand. "Oh, come now, Dagsbrún. Do you not find my company most pleasurable?"

Do you not desire me?

She was in his head once more. Her eyes were wide and hypnotic, drawing him to her side. The room grew hazy, blotting out the fire and the walls until all he could see was her. He strode across the room and sank to his knees beside her. Taking her hand, he held it to his chest.

"I have no heart, Bearla. I cannot desire, only consume, and destroy."

She leaned toward him, her eyes flashing. "And yet, you desire her."

He shook his head. "No. I wish to bestow on her deep affection and shelter her from the likes of you and your brother."

Bearla gripped his shoulders. "Forget her. Forget the ugly halfling and take me instead! I do not need forbindelse with you, only to possess you!"

He threw her back against the cushions. "So that is what this is all about. You want to break the forbindelse."

She dug her fingernails into his shoulders. "I do not know what you mean."

Dagsbrún wanted to rip the limbs from her body. Her whole being oozed with malice and contempt. "Rioghail and you would break it to destroy Anda's chances to bring peace. Because you both know she is the key. And with me by her side, she is unstoppable."

"You do not know that," she snarled. "You do not know what the key is to unlock her power to bring peace."

"We will discover that tomorrow in Naofa, and then we will leave you and your brother behind. And when Anda is successful, the names of Rioghail and Bearla will be forgotten."

Bearla snarled. "You will not escape. Not this time. I could call the guards and have you thrown into the deepest dungeon."

He chuckled. "Yes, yes, and you have a dragon. But even you know the law. No elf must slander another. For an elf's character is second to none." He wrenched himself free of her grasp. "Though I must say that law was most certainly written before your time. For you care nothing for your character, nor the goodwill of those around you."

Bearla screamed and produced a small dagger from under the cushion. She plunged it into Dagsbrún's chest. "I despise you!" she cried, her hands clinging to the hilt of the dagger.

Dagsbrún did not take his eyes off her face. He wrapped his hands around hers and pushed the dagger further into his chest. "You cannot kill me, Bearla. I am already dead." He leaned down and ran a finger lightly over her lips. "Look at me. Memorize me and all you will never have." Still holding her hands onto the hilt, he pulled it out and threw her down. "For I belong to another."

Bearla bit her lip in bitterness. "Does she know that?"

"Does it matter?"

He turned to walk out of the room and then turned back and looked at her one last time. "Know this Bearla. I do not pretend to know anything about affection or compassion or even feelings of the heart. But I do know this. Even being a bit wrong with someone is better than being perfect on your own. That is forbindelse—connecting despite all the obstacles in our path." He bowed curtly. I will see you at sunrise in Naofa.

Chapter 18

They did not see one another until the next morning. Each had fled to their rooms and slammed the door, hoping to shut out the memory of their night. When dawn came, guards escorted them into the courtyard in silence. Vandre saw them and quickly brought Droime. He quickly picked up on the tension.

"I am guessing you had a long night?"

Anda and Dagsbrún said nothing.

An elven guard motioned them to follow. They fell in line behind him, leaving the palace behind and walking down the narrow road toward Naofa Forest. The forest rose before them like a wooden monument to the elvish kingdom. Trees older than time dug their roots deep into the earth and stretched their branches high into the skies, creating a leafy canopy over its guests.

In its woods dwelt the Ardamhains. The high ones of the elvish race. These were the healers, the ancients who knew the secrets of their race. They were the philosophers and the masters of wisdom. The Ardamhains dwelt beneath the tree of Dhia, a giant rowan tree positioned precisely in the middle of the forest in a clearing. Here was the elves' mecca, their most sacred place. The Ardamhains lived and learned entwined in the roots of the tree, learning from its ancient wisdom.

As they approached the tree, they saw that the Eldern were already there. Rioghail was speaking with one of the Ardamhains, and both seemed incredibly agitated. Bearla and the other Eldern sat in chairs made from the woven branches of trees along with six other Ardamhains.

Anda glanced at Dagsbrún, who caught her eye. She blushed and looked away. "Did you have a lovely evening?" she muttered.

Dagsbrún chuckled. "Indeed. It was quite lovely watching you throw yourself at Rioghail."

Anda gritted her teeth. "Why thank you," she replied sarcastically. "As it was watching you chase after Bearla like a wayward pup."

"I was not cashing after her," he hissed.

"It looked quite different from where I was sitting," she replied.

"You hardly sat. A private interlude with Rioghail was much more important!"

"As was stealing a dance from Bearla." She turned at looked at him directly. "Was it just a dance, Dagsbrún? Or did you steal more than that from her?"

He clenched his fists at his side. "And what was Rioghail's gift of choice to you? His company? Or something more?"

She raised her fist to strike him, but he pushed her arm down. "Do not think me as base as you," she said under her breath.

He gripped her hand tightly. "No. That is for Rioghail to think."

As if he heard his name, Rioghail crossed the clearing to them. He bowed slightly and then motioned for them to follow him. As they walked, he turned to gaze over his shoulder at Dagsbrún. "Did you enjoy the festivities last night?" he asked.

Dagsbrún growled. "Did you?"

Rioghail chuckled. "Quite. They were most illuminating."

"It always is wonderful when one can enjoy their own party."

Rioghail turned his head to look at Anda. "Indeed."

"And did you get what?"

Rioghail laughed again. "Did you?"

They reached the trunk of the rowan tree under which the Eldern and Ardamhains sat. Rioghail took his place beside the Ardamhain he had previously been speaking with. The Ardamhains looked at Anda and then took his seat.

"Ciallmhar," Rioghail spoke to the Ardamhain. "Before you are Dagsbrún, whom I am sure you are familiar with, and Anda from... well I do not really know where she comes from." He smirked at Anda and then took his seat.

The Ardamhain known as Ciallmhar motioned for Anda to come closer. "Do you know who I am, child?" he asked.

She shook her head. "No, milord."

He smiled, his eyes twinkling with kindness. "There is no need for formalities, child. I am but a humble teacher, a servant of these woods. You may call me Ciallmhar, and nothing more."

"Thank you," she bowed her head.

Ciallmhar leaned back in his chair. "Rioghail here thinks you and your companions are a menace to our world. Should I believe him?"

Anda lifted her head and squared her shoulders. "No, milord... Ciallmhar, you should not. I come from the world of humans, but I have been taught by the wise elf, Gammel. And he has foreseen the destruction of this world and mine."

Ciallmhar nodded. "Yes, that is what Rioghail tells me. But why should we believe you?"

"Do you think me the sort to lie?"

A smile crossed the Ardamhain's face. "I do not know what sort you are." He stood to his feet. "But the tree will."

Anda blinked. "The tree?"

He nodded. "The tree." He stood and offered her his hand. "This tree has been here since our world was created. Dhia planted the seed himself. It is said that his tears watered it, and his joy gave it the light needed to grow."

Anda took his hand and followed him to the tree's immense trunk. Its bark was ragged and worn and full of nobs and hollows. "It has been here since the dawn of time?"

Ciallmhar placed his hand on the trunk. "It is a storehouse of our histories and people. It judges our worth based on our merit. And, in times such as this, it serves as our judge and our prophet."

"How so?"

He turned and looked at her. Anda thought that his eyes reminded her very much of her father's. "It appears that we are at an impasse. Rioghail wants you and Dagsbrún driven out, but I believe what you say about being given the extraordinary task of bringing peace."

Anda was relieved. "You believe me?"

He nodded. "I do. But for the elves to fully support you, they must see the Dhia Tree find you worthy."

She did not understand. "How do I know if I have its approval?"

He smiled. "It will tell you."

She looked at the tree and then back at Ciallmhar. "The tree talks?"

The clearing erupted in laughter, and Anda's face grew warm. The Ardamhain sensed her discomfort and held up his hand. "Enough!" he shouted. He looked back at Anda. "It talks." He put his hand over his heart. "In here." Taking her hand, he placed it on the tree.

"Ciallmhar," Rioghail shouted. "We grow weary of this tedious gathering!"

Ciallmhar turned back to look at Rioghail, his eyes no longer twinkling, but flashing fire. "You will silence yourself in this place, I say what will and will not be!" The clearing grew silent as he placed his gnarled hand over Anda's. "Breathe, child."

Anda inhaled deeply.

"Breathe and think of nothing but here. Now. Open your mind to the Dhia Tree as you would open a door to a friend."

She closed her eyes and thought of nothing but the surface of the tree's trunk. She pushed her hand hard against its bark, feeling its rugged surface rub against her palm. Through the darkness, she saw the tree rise before her, alone and solitary, hovering in an empty expanse. In her mind, she knelt at the foot of the tree and looked up at its branches. They swayed in a light breeze, slowly shifting in color from green to silver, and then a radiant gold.

"Why are you here, child?"

Anda knew it was the tree speaking to her, but the voice sounded old and distant, as though it came across time to converse with her. "I do not know why I am here," she responded. "Only that I was told to come."

"But why did you come?"

Anda did not know what she was supposed to say. "I do not understand."

"Do you not see your purpose?"

She felt tears welling in her closed eyes. "I do not feel as though I have a purpose. I believe myself to be quite at the whim of whoever is telling me what they wish of me. And while I do not mind it, I simply do not understand it.

The breeze grew stronger, lifting the leaves from the branches and enveloping Anda in them. Then the wind faded away, and the tree was no longer there. In its stead stood an elf cloaked in a robe of green and gold. He looked at Anda as though he had known her all his life.

And to Anda, she somehow believed he had, though she was certain she had never seen him before. And yet, there was an air of familiarity about him that she could not place. She tilted her head to one side and conjured a guess.

"You are... Dhia?"

He smiled at her. "Most perceptive for someone who does not think she has a purpose."

Anda blushed. "You think me too sensitive?"

His body erupted in a long fit of laughter, causing her to feel even more self-conscious. "Oh, my child, your sensitivity is what makes your heart so beautiful. And it is why you have been chosen."

Her tears now spilled over. "But there are so many who are much more apt to finish whatever task that is asked of them."

"And each of them would do so with pride in their heart. It is why Rioghail, and even Dagsbrún and Gammel would fail. Because in their hearts they would consider themselves a hero." He reached out and touched her chin. "But you, Anda, you think nothing of yourself, and therefore you are everything. You hold within you all that this world and yours must learn to be if they are to survive."

"But what do I hold within myself?"

"Good, Anda," he gripped her hand. "An enormous amount of good. It is not the vampire, nor the

elf, nor even mankind that is breaking the Gréasáin. It is the rotting hearts of those that would control it. Their lust for power and their arrogance has corrupted even the purest of hearts."

Anda nodded. "I suppose I can see that."

"But your heart has always wanted to be understood. And each time someone asks something of you, you give yourself wholeheartedly. And so, it will be you, Anda, that will restore peace."

"But how?" she asked. "No one seems to fully know what to tell me to do."

Dhia turned and looked out into the darkness; his arms clasped behind his back. "You and your party will travel to Dorchadas—the home of the vampires. It will be there that you find the means by which to stop the war."

"What am I to look for?"

"In the pits surrounding Dorchadas lies an ancient weapon known as the Waymaker. The prophecies say that they who wield this sword possess the power to command both vampire and elf, thereby ceasing their millennia-long battle."

"Am I to lead a battle with it?"

Dhia shook his head. "No. However, you will surely have to fight for your life and the life of those closest to you. When you find it, take it to the Cleite Tree, the vampire's version of the Dhia Tree. Plunge it into the base of the tree and that will be a sign to elf and vampire alike that the one to unite the two kingdoms has come."

Anda felt overwhelmed. After learning to control her magic, she thought that nothing would surprise her. Now a tree turned elf was telling her to find a prophetical sword and plunge it into yet another tree. She wondered if that tree would also turn into a being.

"You look confused, child."

She shook her head. "No," she replied. "I mean yes, I am struggling to understand. But I do feel as though what you say seems right. As though somehow, I have always known what to do."

He smiled. "That is because you have. Deep down. But you did not want to believe in yourself."

The wind picked up and surrounded Dhia with silver and gold leaves. "It is time for you to go now, Anda. Ciallmhar will know you are the one called to bring peace. No one will question you now."

"But how do I make the vampires believe as you have made the elves believe?"

Dhia had all but faded back into the leaves. His voice was distant and once more seemed ages away. "Trust him, Anda."

"Trust who?" she called out.

"The one who loves you."

Chapter 19

Dhia had been right. When Anda had opened her eyes, there was no question that the Eldern and Ardamhain knew what had occurred. They were silent, with their heads bowed, unmoving in contemplation. Anda had pulled her hand away from the Dhia Tree and fallen against Ciallmhar. He caught her and gently sat her down.

"Did you see him?" he asked.

She nodded. "I saw him."

Dagsbrún had knelt beside her. "Do you have your answers now?"

She had turned to look up at him, searching his face with more questions in her mind. "We go to Dorchadas."

Dagsbrún had frozen. "Dorchadas?"

She stood to her feet. "You are going home."

They had left a short while later after being given supplies by the elves. Rioghail and Bearla had curtly nodded a farewell but stood at a distance. Anda guessed they had been warned by Ciallmhar not to stir up any more trouble.

As she had left, Ciallmhar had kissed her gently on the forehead. "If you ever have need of us, we are at your service."

She had looked over at the Rioghail, whose eyes were locked on her like a hawk. "But would your prince come?" she questioned.

Ciallmhar had laughed. "Rioghail will do what is best for Rioghail. To not come to your aid would make him look like a coward and a fool. He will come. Though his motives would be purely for his own benefit." He had gripped her hand. "Go now and do what you were destined to do."

The journey to Dorchadas had been uneventful. Dagsbrún sensed the presence of elfin trackers in the hills above them and knew their presence kept the vampires from attacking. But he knew they were watching their every move as they drew near the vampire capitol. He knew they could sense him as he sensed them. Their minds and deadened hearts were all linked by the need to satisfy their undying appetites.

He knew their welcome would be tepid at best. He only half-belonged to Dorchadas, and he had not been home since the day his parents were killed. There was little he knew or remembered of his birthplace, save what he had seen in his dreams.

The only way to enter the vampire lands was through a narrow passage between two razor-sharp mountains. They walked single filed through the narrow space in silence, each lost in their own thoughts. Even Droime kept his thoughts from Anda. The passageway at last opened and they found themselves on a plateau overlooking the entirety of Dorchadas.

It was a dark and barren wasteland, marked with blackened trees and jagged rock formations. There was an endless chorus of ravens calling to one another, their eyes flashing in the reddish light. Dagsbrún squared his shoulders and led them down the steep pathway to the valley floor.

"Why do they scream so?" Anda asked, covering her ears.

Dagsbrún smiled wryly. "They are the messengers. They are announcing our arrival. By the time we reach the castle, the entirety of Dorchadas will know we are here."

"What is the castle like?"

"Castle Scath?" Dagsbrún shrugged. "I do not remember it."

"What do you remember?"

He looked off into the distance as if he saw something there he had forgotten. "I remember my mother's face."

"How?" Vandre asked. "You were an infant when..."

"Vandre!" Anda glared at him.

Vandre shrank back. "Sorry."

Dagsbrún shook his head. "I do not know how I remember her face, only that I do. She was the antithesis of my father—delicate, warm, and kind. Whereas he was composed of brute strength and a forcible rage that ran across the land like a thunderstorm. And yet..." He smiled. "And yet she tempered him."

"I suppose that is what love does," Anda replied softly. "Calms the storm."

Her tone caught him off guard. He had become accustomed to her trite remarks and her brusqueness. Her gentle tone almost unnerved him more than her challenging him at every turn.

Castle Scath was unlike the elfish seat of power in every way. Here, shadows ruled, and darkness reigned. There was no grandeur, only defined lines etched in slate. The castle was carved out of a mountain, embedded for centuries in earth and memory, impenetrable to any save those who were issued an invitation.

As they approached, a solitary sentry stepped out of a towering onyx gate. At first, Anda thought that a single guard was strange, but then realized that truly no one would dare come to this place unless it was necessary.

Dagsbrún turned to speak to Anda. "Please, let me do all of the talking this time." She opened her mouth to reply, but he stopped her. "No, just do not say anything at all." He turned back to the guard. "We have come to see Wampyr."

The sentry bowed. "You have been expected for quite some time Dagsbrún, son of Raefn. Come." He gestured toward the interior of the castle. "Wampyr awaits."

They followed him through the gate into the castle. The moment they were in, the great gate closed with a resounding thud. Small rays of light showed through cracks and torches lined the wall, but the place was otherwise filled with darkness. Vandre moved up to walk closer to Anda.

"You could not possibly be nervous, could you?" She asked.

He gripped his bow tightly. "Why would you think I am nervous? What is there to be nervous about? We are simply locked in a castle filled with vampires."

She laughed quietly. "You just came from a castle where you were locked in with elves."

"Elves do not eat you for dinner, Anda. Oh, they will stab you, shoot you, maybe even poison you. But they will not eat you." He shivered. "At least Dagsbrún is only part vampire and can be in the sun. These vampires only live in the dark, and that is unnerving."

"It is not the airy grandeur of the elves," she agreed.

"And who is this Wampyr?" Vandre whispered.

She shook her head. "I do not know. The vampire equivalent to Rioghail?"

Vandre groaned. "Lovely. Does this one have a sister too?"

Anda could not help but laugh and was instantly shushed by Dagsbrún's deathly glare. "Let us hope he is an only child," she whispered back.

As they walked down the hallway, the shadows began to materialize as vampires came to gaze at their visitors. Anda observed that while they were not as colorful as the elves in their appearance, they were every bit as well-dressed, though their palette was much darker in nature. They wore gowns and robes of velvet in black, burgundy, and deep purples. Their hair was done simply, pulled back in ribbons or metal bands. Their faces, though colorless, were still beautiful—chiseled like white granite, each perfectly defined and proportioned.

They stood in small groups whispering to one another as Dagsbrún walked by. Anda realized how immense this must be for him to return to his birthplace. What must they think of the long-lost prince returning with a half-elf, kelpie, and human? Would he even be welcomed by this Wampyr. Would they?

The sentry pushed open a well-worn wooden door and ushered them into a small room. The stone floors were covered with faded rugs and the walls were lined with countless lit candles that cast shadows up to the ceiling.

"Wampyr will be with you shortly, milord," the sentry said, and then left the room, shutting the door behind him.

"At least they refer to you with respect," Anda quipped.

"I feel as though it might be sarcasm," Dagsbrún replied.

They stood in silence for a moment and then Vandre blurted out, "Look, this is all fine for you, Dagsbrún. You are one of them. But Anda and I..."

"Are most welcome."

The baritone voice came from above. They looked but could see nothing in the shadows. And then, in the far corner, a shadow moved against the light of the candles, and they saw a figure detach itself from the ceiling and set down on the floor.

Dagsbrún instinctively stepped in front of Anda and bowed low. "Wampyr."

The figure turned and Anda could see that the vampire had the appearance of an older gentleman with shoulder-length silver hair. But his face still looked like that of a youth, and he moved as though he had not yet reached his thirtieth year.

"Dagsbrún," Wampyr replied, crossing to a chair, and placing himself on the arm. "How very unexpected to see you."

Dagsbrún turned to Anda. "Milord…"

"Wampyr, please," the vampire interjected. "After all, you were my godson before your father betrayed us all."

"Another revelation," Vandre whispered. "We are in a room with an agitated vampire godfather."

Dagsbrún ignored the vampire's comment. "Milord, might I have the honor of introducing you to Anda?"

Wampyr waved his hand dismissively. "Yes, yes. We all know about Anda. Savior, heroine, and all that." He reached over to a small table by his chair and removed a small goblet from it. Lifting it to his lips, he studied Anda over the rim. "Reports have been pouring in from scouts about this halfling. And yet none of them spoke about your beauty, Anda." He set the goblet down. "Why do you suppose that is?"

Dagsbrún responded for her. "An oversight, perhaps?"

Wampyr turned his attention back to Dagsbrún. "Is it? Or perhaps an omission?" He stood and crossed to stand in front of them. "After all, which of my scouts would want to share your beauty, if they hoped to kill you themselves."

"Milord," Dagsbrún placed his arm in front of Anda.

"Wampyr."

Dagsbrún sighed. "Wampyr. We have come at the behest of Dhia himself."

Wampyr raised an eyebrow. "The elf demigod? Oh, well that is a privilege. And what does the elf lord want of us lowly vampires?" He looked at Anda once more. "You are quiet for such a pretty face. Come, come. Tell me what Dhia wants of us?"

Anda looked at Dagsbrún, silently asking his permission to speak. He sighed and nodded reluctantly. She turned back to Wampyr. "Dhia has tasked me with retrieving the sword called Waymaker."

There was a brief silence as Wampyr stared at Anda, his eyes unblinking. Then he began to laugh, a low reverberating laugh. He stood once more and began to pace the floor. "How glorious!" he exclaimed.

Anda looked from Dagsbrún to Wampyr, filled with confusion. "I do not understand."

Wampyr continued to chuckle. "Oh, my dear, how naive you are! Tell me, has anyone bothered to share with you exactly where the Waymaker is?"

Her confusion deepened. "No."

"That sword has been buried at the bottom of a pit for centuries. There is no means by which any living creature could possibly reach it. And even if they did, they would likely die trying to come back to solid ground."

Fear began to inch its way across her heart. "I had not been informed," she replied quietly.

Wampyr continued. "But there is so much more! You were granted access to these lands because we have been told you would bring peace. If you fail to retrieve the sword, you will fail in the mission. And once you do, your life and the lives of your companions are forfeit to me."

The fear now engulfed her completely. "Forfeit?"

The vampire's laughter ceased, and his gaze became piercing. "You will belong to me, halfling. And I promise you, I will enjoy... dining with you."

Dagsbrún pushed Wampyr back. "You will not touch her!"

Wampyr clicked his tongue. "Dear godson, what are you up to? Are you following in your father's footsteps? Developing feelings for someone not like you?"

Dagsbrún gripped Wampyr by the throat and lifted him off the ground. "Godfather, you are being dangerously presumptive."

Anda grabbed his arm. "Dagsbrún, please! Harm him, and we stand no chance!"

Dagsbrún was unmoving. "I will not let him harm you."

"He will not!" she protested. "But harm him, and there will be no sword, no tree, and no peace!"

"I could kill him."

Wampyr leered down at him. "Do your best, dear boy. I am already dead."

Dagsbrún threw him down and turned back to Anda. "You are not planning to go through with

this, are you?"

"What choice do I have?" she retorted. "I try, or we all most certainly perish."

"Anda, you cannot," Dagsbrún's voice cracked.

Her eyes flashed. "I can, and I will!" She turned to Wampyr. "I go to retrieve this sword. Now!"

The vampire rubbed his throat. "Would you perhaps like to rest..."

"No!" She pulled on the door handle and then pounded on it. "The last place I rested and dined; I spent the whole night warding off Rioghail's advances."

Dagsbrún whirled around. "You what?"

Anda was angry and flustered. "Do not pretend you did not know. Nor that you care! You certainly did not seem to care, basking in Bearla's arms."

He grimaced. "Anda, I never…"

Wampyr interrupted. "If you want to go, we must go now. The sun is setting, and there

must be witnesses to this impossible feat." He stood and banged on the door. "When you are done, or dead, we feast."

Vandre turned gray. "Feast on what?"

Wampyr ginned. "Precisely." The sentry opened the door and Wampyr stepped through.

Anda followed behind him, but Dagsbrún grabbed her arm. "Anda, Bearla and I…"

She pushed him off. "I do not want to hear it!"

"But…"

"No!" she whirled around, her face inches from his. "I do not want to hear it. I do not want to be lied to with words twisted to fit your own narrative." She tried to hold back the tears. "Dhia told me to trust the one who loved me, and I think he believed that to be you." She turned to follow after Wampyr. "But even someone like Dhia can be wrong."

Dagsbrún stood frozen in place, feeling the heart he was not supposed to have crumble. Vandre and Droime silently walked by him, knowing better than to say anything.

He did not know what to do. Her accusations, her words had wounded him—he, who had always been impenetrable, unmovable. The look in her eyes had told him he regarded as every other human and elf had—as a beast, a monster—something worthy only of a cage. Despite all his efforts to tell her, to show her how he felt, he had failed.

Chapter 20

Anda had been unsure as to what she had imagined when she thought of tar pits. But the actuality of them was far worse than anything her mind could have fathomed. They were situated amidst a clearing of blackened trees, charred by some unknown fire. The smell was overwhelming. An aroma of oil and smoke, bitter and acidic. She could scarcely bear to breathe air into her lungs.

As they approached the pits, Vandre walked beside her. "I know you think you must do this, but exactly how do you think you are going to succeed?"

"I do not know."

"You do not know?"

"Truthfully, I had not thought to plan this far ahead."

Vandre threw up his hands. "Lovely!"

The word had spread that a halfling elf was going to attempt to retrieve the ancient sword, and the vampires had gathered en masse. They stood around the pit, hands gravely clasped in front of them. Anda could hear their whispers and knew they all had come to watch her fail.

As she reached the edge of the pits, she looked over her shoulder. Dagsbrún was nowhere to be seen. She winced thinking of how harsh she had been to him. It was no wonder that he had not followed her. And still, his absence made her feel incredibly vulnerable.

She felt a nuzzle on her shoulder and turned to see Droime standing beside her. She reached up and stroked his mane, burying her face in it.

What am I doing? she asked.

What you were called to do, he replied.

I will fail.

You will succeed.

I do not know how to succeed.

Use what you have been given and be who you truly are.

She lifted her face from his mane and looked the kelpie in the eyes. She saw herself in their reflection and marveled at how she did not recognize herself. Was any of this worth the struggle? Had she hidden her magic, she would still be home, living a life that was simple and forgettable.

And yet, she knew even looking at her tired reflection in Droime's eyes, that that was a life she could never truly desire. It would be far too tiresome to live doing nothing at all. She could not deny that she was born to cause chaos.

Her revelations were disrupted by Wampyr as he jumped down from a rocky outcropping. "Your presence here has caused quite the stir," he exclaimed. "And surprisingly, the odds are fairly even."

"Odds for what?"

"About whether you will live or die," Vandre interjected.

Wampyr chuckled his unnerving baritone laugh once more. "Incredibly intuitive for a human." He pulled Anda toward the tar pits. "Well, now is as good a time as any."

She stared out over the churning mass, oozing and bubbling like a cauldron over a fire. The pits made a sound that sounded as though the tar were choking on itself. She looked at Wampyr. "I do not suppose you would give me any suggestions?"

He looked at her for a split second and then grabbed her by the arm and pushed her in. "Do not die!"

The tar wrapped itself around her legs, sucking them down. She struggled to keep her balance and not fall face-first into the soupy mess. She unbuckled her sword from her side and turned to throw it back to shore, not wishing to be burdened by it.

Wampyr caught it, only to have a hand reach out and pull it from his fingers. He turned to see that the hand belonged to his godson. Dagsbrún wrenched the sword from his fingers and held it to his chest. He then turned and watched Anda struggle further out into the pit.

"It is a lost cause, you know," Wampyr clasped his hands behind his back.

"I should think you would hope it is not," Dagsbrún replied. "If she fails, the elves will be upon you before you blink. And in a fight, Rioghail would likely win."

"In a fair fight, yet. I do not play fair."

Dagsbrún sighed. "One of the reasons the world is crumbling." He turned and looked at his godfather. "You stand to lose as much as anyone. If there cannot be reconciliation, then there will be war. And if you lose that war, the vampires will question your ability to lead. It is quite easy to be in control when there is no one challenging you."

"The elves have been challenging me for years."

"In skirmishes, yes. This would bring them to your door."

Wampyr changed the subject. "And what will happen to your halfling if she is successful?"

"She is not my halfling."

The vampire chuckled. "Your thoughts tell me otherwise. If she brings peace like you so ardently wish, do you think she will give you a second thought? She will be lauded as a hero, set above even Rioghail. You will still just be a half-breed. Half a creature of the night, half of the light."

Dagsbrún stiffened. "Be that as it may, Anda has taught me that the world is more than just ourselves. She has left everything that is familiar, to help a world that drove her mother away. I admire that immensely."

Wampyr's expression softened softly. "This world killed both your parents."

Dagsbrún nodded. "Yes, and I would like to see that senselessness end." He looked out at Anda. "She can change it. She can alter nature itself."

Anda trudged through the tar, inch by aching inch. Her lungs were filled with the tar's pungent stench, its smokey bitterness stinging her eyes. She knew she must keep walking but could not think where she was walking to. She realized this task was quite literally impossible. There was no feasible way to find anything in this muck, much less a sword. Her chest tightened, and her eyes grew blurry.

She knew was going to fail.

Anda reached out and grabbed onto a rock. Clinging to it, she pulled herself out of the tar, her lungs searching for clean air, but finding none. She laid her head against the rock and burst into tears. Of all the ways she had imagined herself dying, this was most certainly not one of them.

Anda, do not surrender to your fear.

She heard Droime's voice and looked back across the tar toward the shore, but the vapors blocked her view. She gasped for air, choking on the fumes she inhaled. *Droime, I have nothing left. It is quite impossible.*

There is nothing you cannot do, Anda.

I can't...

What would Gammel do?

Anda gasped. *He would do what he was made to do.* Her eyes widened. *He would use his magic.*

A whinny traveled across the tar to her ears. *You claimed a kelpie, now claim the sword. Claim you were born to be.*

Anda inhaled once more, finding the last remaining bits of clean air, and then lowered herself back into the mire. She looked back at the shore and could vaguely make out the figures watching her. There was Droime, Vandre... and Wampyr. And then, standing behind him she could almost make out...

Dagsbrún.

He was here... there. He had come. Her words had not cut so deeply as to cause his total rejection. His presence gave her courage. "Use the magic," she whispered. "Use the magic, claim the sword."

She closed her eyes. The tar, the rocks, and the spectators on the shore all faded from view. She reached out and thrust her hand into the tar. She was no longer standing in the oppressive muck but on an empty plane, void of anything but herself. She swept her arm out in front of her, and the air became a bit more breathable. Inhaling, she called out to the sword, willing it to her as she had done with Droime. The empty space before her erupted in a myriad of colors, blended in watery magnificence.

Shifting through the colors, she saw it. Wedged beneath a rock a few feet away. Waymaker. Her body did not feel as though it were weighted down by any form of matter. She reached toward the sword and watched it writhe and twist against the imprisonment of the rock. She stretched her fingers out to the point of breaking, willing the sword to come, but it was firmly embedded in its resting place.

She lowered her hand and crossed to where the sword lay. Wrapping her fingers around the hilt of the sword, she felt a searing jolt of heat course through her body. The sword began to twitch about with increasing violence, trying to break free of its prison. She set her foot against the base of the rock and pulled with all her might.

There was a great scraping sound and Anda pulled the sword free. It clanked to the ground with an echoing thud. She stared at the sword for only a moment before turning back toward the shore. As she walked, the colors began to fade and the air around her thickened. Slowly she became aware that she was no longer walking but fighting to wade through the tar. She held the sword above the mire but could scarcely keep her head free.

She became aware of shouting on the shore, as she became even more aware that her strength was gone. Her arms and legs were trapped and as she fought, she began to sink lower. Her lungs were consumed with the pungent odor. Darkness began to ink out her vision. She held the sword toward the shore, wishing for someone to take it and relieve her of its heavy burden. As the tar crept over her mouth and nose, she thought she heard wings overhead, but resigned herself to accept that it was only the winds of finality. She floated into unconsciousness, amused that oblivion was not quite as horrific as she had dreamt it would be.

Dagsbrún had watched Anda fight her way through the tar filled with terror. Every muscle, every sinew in his body pulled taut with tension. He fought every urge to hasten to her side and pull her out. Vandre had pulled him back when she had plunged beneath the surface of the tar, only to reemerge with Waymaker in her hand. She had fought her way back to shore, but her strength was gone.

He waited until he saw her sink below the surface, and then spread his wings and hurled himself across the surface of the tar. Reaching down, he gripped the tip of the sword and pulled. The tar held fast to Anda, and he strained against it. Slowly, he lifted her out until at last, she was free. He cradled her in his arms, laying the sword across her chest.

Laying her down on the ground, he handed the sword to Vandre. He fell to the earth beside her, gently cradling her head. His fear overtook him as he looked down at Anda. She was covered in tar, her clothes and hair slick with its oily residue. He tenderly wiped her face and pulled her close.

"Anda?" he whispered. "Anda, can you hear me?"

Vandre sank down beside him. "Dagsbrún... I do not think she..."

"No!" Dagsbrún pushed him away and turned back to Anda. "No." He felt water on his face and realized his eyes were filled with tears. He gripped her tightly and pulled his wings up, enveloping them in a feathery cocoon.

"Anda? Please. Please, this cannot be the end."

She was unmoving, her skin white under the black tar.

He frantically kissed her hair. "I never betrayed you, Anda. Bearla wanted me to, but there has never been anyone but you. Not since the first time I laid eyes on you." He let out an agonizing scream. "You cannot capture my deadened heart, only to leave me alone!" He placed his forehead against hers and wept. "Please," he begged. "Come back."

And her heart heard him.

Anda gasped, breathing in life. Dagsbrún lowered his wing and lifted her in his arms. "I have you," he whispered in her ear.

Anda laughed weakly. "I could have done it myself."

Dagsbrún smiled. "Of that, I have no doubt."

Wampyr approached them, his eyes wide with amazement. "Never in all my long life have I seen something like that."

Dagsbrún turned toward the castle. "We must get her clean and warm."

Wampyr nodded. "The castle is yours. I stand humbled. She truly is incredible."

Dagsbrún looked down at her. "Indeed. Incredible, and rare." His voice softened. "And the tragedy is, she does not know it."

Chapter 21

The night turned into day and crawled on for an eternity, only to fade into another night. Dagsbrún had carried Anda back to the castle as she slipped in and out of consciousness. He had called for water and rags and gently removed as much of the tar from her body as he could. He had taken a brush and ran it through her hair, removing each tangle. Then he had wrapped her in a robe and laid her in a bed.

He stood by her door, ever vigilant as she fell in and out of consciousness. Sometimes she cried out, other times she moaned, never fully awakening. His heart would not cease to pound. It was broken, bleeding, but still pounding relentlessly in his chest. The agony of watching her nearly drown and now cling to life had awoken in him an acute awareness of how desperately he longed for her.

How he loved her.

His eyes saw her in all her virtue, her tender heart, and her selfless desire to do whatever was asked of her. She was wild in spirit, but gently in nature. In his mind, she had been treated as an abomination by so many, and yet was the epitome of all that he believed to be good and beautiful.

When she had come to Castle Skog, he had longed to possess her, and yet now, there was nothing he would do to set her free. He knew he could have entered her mind, taken control of her body and spirit, and kept her as a plaything. But she had shown him her true self and that trust caused him to want nothing more than to protect her until his body let out its last breath.

And yet, here he was, helpless yet again to save her. She should have healed herself by now, as she did back at Castle Skog, but she still lay in a restless, fitful sleep. As time dragged on, the length and fervor of his pacing increased. He was an animal caged, trapped by his inadequate ability to help her.

His worry wore on him late into the night. At long last he could bear it no more and gently opened the door to her room. She lay sleeping, her hands spread out across her pillow, her hair cascading down over her shoulders like a fiery blaze. He could hear her heart beating steadily like the distant roll of thunder.

Dagsbrún sat down on the edge of the bed. Gently, he moved a stray strand of her away from her eyes. "Do you know what a wonder you are?" he whispered.

She stirred, turning her head towards him and he pulled back. Her eyes opened, first only slightly and then darting open wide. She bolted upright in the bed, gasping for air. "I cannot breathe!" She screamed. "I cannot breathe!"

He instinctively reached out and gripped her tightly. "It is all right. You are all right."

Her breathing slowed, and she pulled her head back to look at him. "The sword... Did I?"

He smiled. "All is well, Anda. The sword is with Vandre and Droime. You have won the respect of the Wampyr and the vampires, which is not a small feat. You have done it."

She pulled back a bit more. "You came." Her brow furrowed. "I did not think you would."

Dagsbrún gently cupped her hand in his. "I would not have missed you plunging through tar for the world."

Anda tilted her head to one side as though she were trying to remember something. "I thought I had drowned. I was suffocating. I could not breathe. And then," she looked at Dagsbrún. "Then I heard wings." Her expression softened as she realized what he had done. "Did it hurt?"

He shrugged. "Not much." He stood to his feet. "Not as much as it did to think you would not live to see another day."

Anda lowered her eyes. "I am sure you would have survived."

Dagsbrún walked around the end of the bed. "Anda, had you died, there would be no reason to exist. I was born half-dead, the only heartbeat I ever had was my mother's. And even that was taken from me. But then you came to Castle Skog and the bleakness of my world was painted with color."

Anda's eyes remained lowered, but he could see her lip quiver. "I did nothing."

"You did everything! You thought me a monster, and a monster I am. But you saw more than just demons. You looked into me and found my soul."

She looked up at him, tears brimming in her eyes. "Truly, there has not been a moment since that night on the castle roof, when you have not possessed my mind."

He reached his hands out to embrace her but then pulled back as though he had touched something hot. He tried to turn from her, but she grabbed his arm. Before her fingers came to fully rest on his skin, he had gripped her hand. "I cannot let you care for me. It would be wrong."

Anda was taken aback. "What do you mean, you cannot let me?" She could feel her face grow warm. "I was not aware it was your choice."

Turning back, his face brushed against hers. "Anda, I could destroy you. So help me, I want to hold you, search out all of your secrets, and know what it is to belong to, and with someone. But one weak moment, and I could rip you to ruin."

Her heart was pounding, and she knew he heard it. She moved toward him, only for him to shrink back. "You told me once, I needed to ask you."

He held his hands up. "Please, do not."

"Dagsbrún, I am asking."

He sank to the floor. "But Anda, I am a monster and a beast. I am my demon's puppet. Nothing good could come from this."

She smiled tenderly. "How wonderful would it be to have something finally worth losing? I have never believed that to exist before."

He hung his head. "I have done terrible things."

She touched his head. "Let me love you anyway."

Dagsbrún could not bear the thought of harming her. He leaped to his feet and moved further across the room. "I am darkness!" he screamed. "I will envelop you in it!"

All her emotions ruptured from her soul. She wiped her tears away angrily. "It is so easy to love the light. That is what we are told to do. Love the sun because it brings life. Love the sunrise because we are told it is beautiful." She clenched her hands. "Show me your darkness, Dagsbrún. I do not want you without your darkness. I ask you, as you told me I needed to. Please, I love you too much to change you."

Time hung suspended over them like a storm waiting to break. Dagsbrún thought of all the ways in which Anda could die at his hand… and then, all the ways she could die if he were not there to protect her. He saw the depth of her heart, and it made his dead one burst. It pounded down the walls he had built in his mind and gave his feet wings.

In an iota of a second, she was wrapped in his arms. So suddenly that all manner of breath left her. He looked through the windows of her eyes and saw their future, an abundance of laughter, love, and moments that spiraled into infinite memories. He lowered his head and brushed his lips against hers. She was overpowering.

Anda could no longer stand on her own. Her legs gave way, but he held her up. "I have not fallen in love with you because you are good," she whispered. "I have fallen in love with you because in you I see my own darkness. It has a home in you. In you, I have found my light."

He moved his lips to the curvature of her chin. "Ask me again, Anda. Ask me, and I will yield."

The corner of her lips turned upward. "I am asking you to yield."

His voice was low and hoarse. "Ask me to kiss you. Ask me and let the only name on your lips ever be mine."

Anda could not feel her body. She could not feel the coldness of the room, or the weight of the robe on her shoulders. All she could feel was him, filling up everything, everywhere.

"Kiss me."

The world caught fire. It erupted in a soaring ecstasy that set the star spiraling through the heavens. Every moment of agony, every memory of sadness, dissipated as their souls drank in the touch of one another. Their skin ignited with electricity, every nerve ricocheting across the surface.

Dagsbrún turned from her lips to the hands that held his face. "Every inch of you is a wonder."

She sighed. "I wish we could disappear. Blend into one another, and then vanish. Let the world be without us for one night."

He ran his lips over the inside of her arm. "We could run away."

Anda fought everything within her that screamed in agreement. "But then we would make one another lesser than what we are called to be."

"I could never be less of a being than what I am when I am with you."

"Nor I, with you," she pulled away slightly. "But we must finish what we began. I must take Waymaker and find this tree. I must put an end to it all."

"*We* must put an end to it all," he pulled her back. "Anda…"

She heard her name like a plea for salvation. Pushing herself up on her toes she touched his lips with hers. They were soft but filled with desperation and longing. A longing to be redeemed in her arms. She gripped the back of his head and held him close, willing him to forget the nightmares that had haunted him.

Her robe fell to the ground and the breeze sent a chill up her legs under her shirt. She shivered and he pulled her tightly to him. She felt his fire, the alchemy between them, like lightning through the heart. His lips, cold in one breath like the first snow, turned hot like melted honey in the next.

Dagsbrún fought himself. He cascaded over waves of relief and delight. She loved him. *Him*. The monster, the beast. She loved all of him. All his faults, his weaknesses, she loved him despite his rage and anger. She loved him despite his thirst for blood and his longing to prey. How could she? He could not fathom it. As he kissed her lips, he willed himself to believe that it was not true, that it was all a dream, a beautiful, longing dream… but she was more real than the room in which they stood.

His lips touched her forehead and laughed softly. "Not the forehead." She touched her lips. "Down here."

He smiled. "A kiss on the forehead is for the soul." He cupped her chin and kissed her once more on the lips. "A kiss on the lips is my love pouring out of me into your heart."

As he pulled away to look at her, he noticed a bluish hue surrounding her face like an ethereal halo. The light danced with bits of gold, radiating off her face and sparking outward.

He took her hand and held it up. It too shone with the same light. "Anda, you are radiating."

Her eyes widened. "What is it?" She turned her hand to and fro in the light.

Dagsbrún clasped her hand to his chest. "Anda," he said through his tears. "It is forbindelse."

"Forbindelse?" she could not believe it. She touched her face. "I did not think it would be like this."

Dagsbrún picked her up and spun her around, the blue light scattering like stardust. "You are alight with it!" He set her down and kissed her once more, their souls meeting on one another's lips. "It makes sense now," he exhaled his joy. "Gammel said it was meant to be, but I did not think it possible." He kissed her again, seeing her thoughts, her every emotion and feeling. "This is why Rioghail and Bearla tried to make us doubt and betray one another."

A second kiss caused her to gasp. There was redemption in his lips like a hand pulling from drowning, scooping her up, and giving her an abundance of air. She stepped back, her face warm with joy. "I can hear your soul."

He laughed. "You mean my heart? Though I do not know how. It barely beats."

She lay her head on his chest. "No, your soul. It sounds like the melting of snow into a stream." She pressed her ear closer to his chest. "Like the beat of a hundred hummingbirds wings." She ran her hands down his arms and gripped her hands. "It is composing our own song to dance to."

She pulled him to the middle of the floor and stepped around him, moving to a song he could not hear, still clasping his hands. As she did, the light moved over her in a gentle stream and onto him. It encircled his arms, entwined his neck, and crowned his head. He leaned down and kissed her again.

"So many kisses," she said.

"I give you my love in these kisses," he breathed into her ear. "And you give one in return. And in that exchange, neither one of us loses anything… but gains everything."

"Kiss me again," she replied breathlessly. "And make me immortal."

To which he replied, "Your love will last for eternity, and I, by your side."

Chapter 22

The night seemed eternal and yet was all too fleeting. As the sun rose and the vampires sunk into their dark corners, Dagsbrún pulled Anda from her sleep. They had sat together late into the night, watching the stars dance across the sky until at last Anda had laid her head in Dagsbrún's lap and drifted off into a peaceful sleep.

He had watched her sleeping, still in disbelief that she loved him. He watched her chest rise and fall, and her mouth turn up in a crooked smile as she dreamed. Her hair fell across his legs in a crimson cascade, and marveled at her hair held such a myriad of shades of red. There was the red of apples as they came into their prime in the Fall and the red of dying embers dancing in a fire. There was the red of the last moments of sunset, and the red of lips.

Lips like hers. When he had kissed those lips, he had seen infinite time pass through his eyes, and in the same moment, eternity stood still. Never in all his hundreds of years had he wished for time to last forever. Before her, it had been a senseless strand of preying and hunting and killing. He had looked at his life and seen nothing but futility. His reckless, wild behavior had reflected his sense of complete helplessness in ever finding any sense of purpose in his life. And the more he had killed and watched the life pass out of his victim's eyes, the more he had wished for his own demise. But how could he look toward something that could never be? For there was little that could kill an elf, much less a vampire. Indeed, his only true weakness was the silver-tipped arrows of the elves.

Until Anda, there had never been any purpose in existence. But now she had given him direction. She had created a watercolor tapestry of radiance with her presence. And loving her was indeed the only masterpiece he ever wished to create.

And so, stirring her to consciousness, filled him with dread. For what would the day hold? She must take the sword to the Cleite Tree and plunge it into its trunk. And then, who knew what would happen after that? Dhia had said it would bring peace, but peace at what cost? And when? A split second after, or longer?

He brushed his finger along her cheek, and she turned her face toward him. She opened her eyes and smiled, remembering where she was. Stretching her arms out, she touched his face.

"Hello."

Dagsbrún smiled. "Hello."

Sitting up, she looked out at the sun rising. "It is time then?"

Dagsbrún nodded. "It is."

She stood to her feet and remembered she had only her shirt on. "Do you have any notion as to where the rest of my clothes might be?"

He chuckled softly. "Covered in tar, I am afraid."

Her brow furrowed. "Well, this is a nuisance."

His smile widened. "Never fear. I will find you something." He crossed to the door and pulled it open. "I will be back shortly."

She rushed after him. "Dagsbrún…"

He turned. "Yes?"

"I do not want to be alone."

"You cannot possibly be afraid. You have already done the hard part."

Anda clutched at his arm. "I am afraid. I am always afraid."

He cupped her face. "I will return, and then I will remain by your side."

"Do you promise?"

He stepped outside the room and bowed slightly. "With my life."

Anda had dressed, and they had slipped quietly out of the castle. Dagsbrún knew Wampyr would be roaming the halls somewhere, but he did not care to converse with his godfather. He wanted Anda's task over and done with and for them to disappear somewhere that was not in Dorchadas. They made their way quietly to the stables where Vandre and Droime were sleeping. Vandre had fallen to sleep against Droime, clutching Waymaker to his chest. Awaking them, Anda took Waymaker from Vandre.

"Thank you, dear friend," she said, gently taking the sword from his hands.

"Think nothing of it," he replied, brushing the hay from his pants. "Not everyone can say they have slept with that sword."

They made their way beyond the castle into the light of the morning. Dagsbrún led the way through the trees and pits along a path behind the castle. From there, the path veered up the mountain to a small walled garden. The gate had fallen into disrepair and was partially torn off its rusted hinges. Dagsbrún climbed over the top of the door and helped Anda.

"What is this place?" she asked.

"It once was the Garden of Bhroin," he replied. Wampyr made it for his mate."

"His mate? I did not think him a romantic."

"He was a different sort of vampire back then. He was still a killer, but he loved Realtai. Loved her to the point of near madness. He built this garden for her. They would come here in the moonlight, two lovers lost in their own private paradise."

"And then?"

Dagsbrún sighed. "An elf murdered Realtai. It was senseless and without provocation. They killed her as she sat reading here in the garden."

Anda's brow furrowed. "I can see how that would give Wampyr cause to hate the elves."

He lifted a branch for her to cross under. "The hate passed down to him now was animated in his heart. He laid waste to the garden and has not come here since. The only thing left untouched is the Cleite Tree."

"Because it is sacred?"

He nodded. "Like the Dhia Tree, it ties Dorchadas to the Gréasáin and their ancestors. Long before the dissension between the vampire and elves, it was a meeting place. But that has long since passed."

Anda sighed. "So much hate and anger. And for so long."

"Indeed," he agreed. "And no one truly remembers why the fighting began in the first place."

"Prejudice and hate—the foundation for an awful history."

Dagsbrún looked at her, bemused and impressed with her perception. "It is a wonder you have not lived here your whole life."

She laughed. "Why? Because I understand the nature of most beings? That when one does not understand the other, they draw their own conclusions. And that those conclusions are usually wrong? I have lived that my whole life."

"It has given you character," he replied.

"It has given me a strong desire to be suspicious of everyone." Droime knickered softly behind her. "And I had every right to be suspicious of you," she told the kelpie. "But it makes trusting those worthwhile all the more precious."

The hedges and tangled bramble parted into a clearing. The ground was riddled with dead leaves and wild grasses and had been uncared for quite some time. In the middle of the clearing stood the Cleite Tree—a mammoth oak tree with a wide trunk and gnarled branches that stretched over the dead earth for several feet. The branches were barren and had several knobs and hollows in them. The tree bent and swayed in the wind, sending a haunting moan throughout the garden.

"What is it about elves and vampires and trees?" Vandre mumbled.

Dagsbrún ran his fingers along the rugged patterns on the trunk. "Trees are the closest depiction to the Gréasáin that we have," he replied. "Their roots create webs of life under the earth, drawing in water and nutrients. And their branches stretch out, sharing the tree's life story."

Anda lifted up Waymaker. "But why must the sword go into the tree?"

Dagsbrún turned back to Anda. "The tree is vampire. The sword was made by the elves but stolen by the vampire. It's a union of the two—a meeting of two worlds."

She weighed the sword in her hand. "Which is why it must be the Cleite Tree and not the Dhia Tree."

He nodded. "Precisely."

Anda looked at the tree and then back down at Waymaker. It was heavy in her hands, a burden she carried the weight of throughout her whole body. She sensed the power of the tree and sword and trembled at the idea of the two meeting.

Gripping the hilt, she pointed the blade at the tree. Breathing deeply, she squared her shoulders and dug her heels into the earth. "What do I do?"

A voice answered from the edge of the clearing. "Find the heart of the tree and pierce it there." They turned to see Wampyr standing in the shadow of the trees. His face was protected from the rising sun by the tree branches.

"Wampyr, you should not be here!" Dagsbrún shouted.

Wampyr held up his hand. "I have lived long enough to learn how to walk in the shadows when there is too much light." He raised a hood on the back of his cloak to cover his head and strode across the clearing. "Find the heart." He pointed to the tree. "There, in the exact middle. There is the swords' resting place."

Anda studied the Cleite Tree until she saw it. A darkened mark in the middle of the trunk. She pulled her arms back and aimed the sword at the spot.

Dagsbrún came up behind her and gently gripped her arms. "I would have thought with all your training, you would be able to hit an inanimate object. He gently raised her arms and pointed the sword downward. "Striking at a downward angle will give you more force."

She turned away from the tree and looked up at his face. "I do this, and we have our own lives."

His smile met hers. "And ever after."

Anda, there is danger. Droime's voice interrupted Anda's thoughts.

Not now, Droime.

Anda…

Not now!

She turned her focus back to the tree. As she braced to pierce the tree, she heard what sounded like a tightened harp string being plucked and a rush of wind. Dagsbrún let out a low grunt and stumbled backward.

Anda heard Vandre scream, and Droime let out a piercing shriek. Anda's arms dropped as she felt Dagsbrún let go. Whirling around, she saw Dagsbrún fall to his knees, an arrow protruding from his chest.

"No!"

Anda dropped the sword and rushed to his side. A flurry of arrows sailed across the sky, plunging into the trees and earth. She grabbed Dagsbrún's arms and pulled him behind the Cleite Tree for shelter. Dropping to the ground, she pulled his coat away and examined the arrow.

It was elvish.

Wampyr fell to the ground beside her. "I must get back to the castle and awaken the others. They will be slaughtered otherwise."

Anda grabbed his arm. "You cannot leave us!"

He stood. "Listen to me. You must get that arrow out! It is dipped in silver. It will kill him."

"I cannot!" she screamed. "I do not know how!"

"You can!" he snapped. "Pull. Hard." Wampyr's expression slightly. "Hurt him now or lose him forever." Without another word, he turned and plunged toward the trees on the other side of the clearing. As he reached the edge, a second wave of arrows cascaded into the garden, and Wampyr was hit. He fell into a tree and slumped to the ground.

Anda saw him fall and screamed yet again. She looked about for Vandre and Droime. They had taken shelter a few feet away. She closed her eyes and called out to Droime. *Take Vandre and make haste for the castle. Awake the vampires. They must have a chance to defend themselves.* Droime neighed and nipped at Vandre's tunic. Vandre looked toward Anda, and she motioned for him to go. Without hesitating, he climbed on Droime's back and plunged into the woods.

Dagsbrún clutched at her arm, gasping for air. "Take it out," he choked. "The silver is coursing through my body."

Tears streamed down her face. "I do not know how."

He screamed. "It burns!"

She wiped her face and sat on her knees. Gripping the arrow, she pulled, but the arrow would not budge. She heard feet crashing as elves scaled the wall and jumped into the garden. Looking over her shoulder, she saw thirty elf fighters approaching, their bows laced with drawn arrows. Her heart pounded in her chest as she saw who led them.

Rioghail.

He strode toward them in elvish armor, his bow at the ready. His face was covered in smug arrogance. Anda pulled Dagsbrún against the tree, hiding in its roots. Rioghail passed by them, crossing the clearing to Wampyr.

"What an unexpected surprise," Rioghail sneered.

Wampyr coughed. "I wish I could say the same." He pushed himself up onto his feet. "Forgive me if I do not issue pleasantries, but it appears I have been shot."

Rioghail dropped his bow and drew his sword. "Apology accepted. It appears you do not have much time left."

Wampyr drew his sword. "Pity. I should have liked to watch you die slowly."

Rioghail swung his sword at Wampyr, who blocked his blow. "Instead, I will watch you burn from the inside out."

Wampyr pushed himself away from the tree and lunged at Rioghail. Anda was amazed that he had the strength left to fight at all. But he matched the elf blow for blow.

She turned her attention back to Dagsbrún. His face was ashen, and his veins were straining to fight the poison coursing through his body. Gripping the arrow again, she pulled with all her might but could not make the arrow budge. She fell to the ground beside him, convulsing in tears.

He reached out and touched her face with his hand. "It is no good, Anda. It will not move."

She gripped his hand. "I cannot lose you."

His eyes grew heavy. "You never will."

His hand went limp in hers. She gently let it fall to the ground. Rage filled her. Not like this. This would not be how she lost him. She rolled him onto his back and swung her leg over his side. She wrapped her hands around the arrow and pulled with all her might. Her arms and shoulders exploded with pain, and she continued to pull. "*Nil aon chumhacht agat*[7]," she whispered. "*Nil aon chumhacht agat!*"

And then, slowly, the arrow began to slide outwards. She grimaced as she felt it nick muscle and bone. Anda did not know if she had the strength left to pull more. Dagsbrún screamed in agony, writhing on the ground beneath her, and she tried to shut out his cries.

Digging her heels into the ground, she screamed a third time, "*Nil aon chumhacht agat!*" and pulled the arrow from Dagsbrún's chest. His whole body arched and fell softly to the ground, his eyes closing and his head falling to one side. Anda lay her head on his chest and felt for any movement.

There was none.

Now, her rage consumed her. She reached for Waymaker and used it to push herself to her feet. She turned towards Wampyr and Rioghail. Raising the sword high over her head, she plunged toward them.

"Rioghail!" she screamed.

He turned away from Wampyr, surprise on his face. He raised his sword to meet hers only to feel his chest shatter as

---

[7] Nil aon chumhacht agat means "You have no power" in Gaelic.

Wampyr leaped into the air and plunged his sword downward through Rioghail's neck. The elf's eyes grew wide with shock as he fell to the ground, spewing blood onto the ground. Wampyr kicked him, and he fell to his side, the light fading from his eyes.

Wampyr dropped his sword and fell to his knees. His breath came in short, hoarse gasps. He looked at Anda and muttered hoarsely, "Finish it."

Chapter 23

With rage still seething, Anda turned from the elf and vampire and strode toward the tree. Raising Waymaker, she charged the tree. "For the Vale," she whispered. "For Vandre, for Droime. For Gammel. For my father." Tears filled her eyes. "For my mother. For Dagsbrún!"

Waymaker cut through the heart of the Cleite Tree as though the bark with water. She drove it into the hilt and then let go. The tree erupted in a burst of purple flame that radiated out of its branches into the sky and swept across the ground through its roots. The flame worked its way across the ground, up into the trees, and over the garden wall. The sky turned all the colors of sunset, even though the sun had barely risen in the east.

Anda was thrown backward, her head hitting the ground. Exhaustion took hold of her body. She was unsure as to whether she had even done what she was supposed to do. How was restoring peace meant to present itself like after all? She turned her head toward Wampyr, who was watching the flame flurry through the garden. It swirled about his arms and hands as he held them up in wonder. Anda smiled. At least Wampyr was satisfied. She tilted her head to see Dagsbrún, who remained motionless against the tree. She wanted to lay beside him and lose herself in his arms. She twisted her body around and crawled toward him. Pushing herself up, she leaned against the Cleite Tree and gently laid his head in her lap.

The flame that had burst into the sky now trickled down like soft rain. As it hit the trees and earth, the world erupted in rebirth. The trees furled with delicate green leaves, and the earth sprouted grass bedecked with dew. Blossoms peeked out between cracks in the garden wall as ivy crept over the stones. Even mushrooms sprouted amidst the moss on the bramble and fallen logs.

Anda breathed deeply. "Look what we did," she ran her hands through his hair. "You always knew... You knew I would succeed. You believed in me." The words caught in her throat. "Even when I doubted myself. And now, where are you?" She kissed him fervently. "Dagsbrún, please. Can you hear me?" She pounded his chest. "Do not leave me."

She was met with only silence.

Anda laid her head on his chest and sighed, surrendering to the irony of the world blossoming as her heart was dying. She longed for safety... though she did know where she would ever find that again.

And then, her mind drifted to Gammel. She was quite surprised by it. He entered her thoughts as though issued an invitation. And Anda remembered his promise to her.

If you ever need me, I will be there.

Anda pulled the seeing stone, Asestein, from her pouch. She closed her eyes, thinking she would never open them again, and rubbed the stone absentmindedly. But as she drifted into unconsciousness, she whispered, "I need you."

And then, all went quiet in her head and heart.

The garden was silent save for the swaying branches. The purple light hovered like a canopy over the quiet scene. In the distance, there was the occasional distant shout from the castle, but the garden had fallen into a quiet tomb.

And then the ground began to hum, low and reverberating. It was so quiet in the beginning that the birds that had settled in the freshly blooming trees turned their heads toward the sound, unsure as to whether it was real. But then it grew louder, becoming undeniable that the ground was indeed humming and vibrating. Pebbles and pinecones began to bounce about, and the birds flew to higher branches, now wary of their newfound perches.

It grew louder and louder until it began to sound as though it were more a roar than a hum. The purple hue of the Cleite Tree was replaced with a blinding white light radiating from its core. It filled the garden with its brilliance until the garden was consumed by it. There was an enormous crack, and the light died away.

And there, standing in its stead, was Gammel. His hood was pulled up over his face, and he carried both his staff and a sword. He surveyed his surroundings, sword at the ready, and then when he saw there was no enemy to fight, he sheathed his weapon and knelt beside Anda and Dagsbrún.

He checked her pulse and sighed. "Well done, Anda. You have not managed to die yet." He then turned to Dagsbrún. He examined the wound where the arrow had pierced him and then listened to his chest for breathing. The lines on his face deepened. "You, however, are another story."

Gammel threw his robe to the ground and picked up his staff. He placed the tip of the staff on Dagsbrún's chest and pressed lightly. He bowed his head and began his incantation. "*Gluais cnaimh, agus anail, a 'toirt anail. Tha do thuras fhathast ri shiubhal. Till thugam.*[8]"

---

[8] *Gluais cnaimh, agus anail, a 'toirt anail. Tha do thuras fhathast ri shiubhal. Till thugam!* Means "Bone move, and breath breathe. Your journey is still to be traveled. Return to me" in Gaelic.

Dagsbrún did not move. Gammel gripped his staff and muttered again, *"Gluais cnaimh, agus anail, a 'toirt anail. Tha do thuras fhathast ri shiubhal. Till thugam."*

There was only silence.

"Come back to me, Dagsbrún!" Gammel shouted. "Your time is not yet upon you!" The elf swung his staff three times around his head with his voice echoing like thunder, *Gluais cnaimh, agus anail, a 'toirt anail. Tha do thuras fhathast ri shiubhal. Till thugam!"*

He brought the staff down hard onto Dagsbrún's chest with a resounding crack. Lightning split out from its tip, igniting the garden in a flash of light. The light spiraled outward and faded into the distance, leaving the garden silent save for Gammel's labored breathing.

He dropped the staff and sank next to his grandson. "Come on, boy," he whispered. "There is too much love for you here." He wiped away dirt from Dagsbrún's face, tears filling his eyes. "Not yet. Not like this."

And then the earth began to hum once more, and the purple light that had hovered around them now began to contract and swirl about Dagsbrún's body. Gammel sat back on his heels, his eyes wide with wonderment.

"That's it," he panted. "Beautiful Gréasáin, work your wonder around him!"

The light continued to contract, gathering under and around Dagsbrún. It settled on his body in delicate bunches, resting on the surface of his skin. As Gammel watched, the light sank into Dagsbrún's body, lighting it from within. It traveled through the lines in his hands, the arch of his forehead, and the sinews in his neck, traveling toward his heart. The light gathered into an orb, pulsing, and compressing. Its power pulled Dagsbrún from the ground and worked its way through his body.

And then, there was one final pulse, and the light shot through him, catapulting into the sky, and sending Dagsbrún crashing back to the earth. The light dissipated back into the ground, leaving Gammel in awe of what he had just beheld.

He leaned forward and gripped Dagsbrún's face in his hands. "Come on, lad," he muttered.

Dagsbrún heaved and convulsed and rolled to one side, gasping for air. Gammel threw his arms around him, sobbing, and Dagsbrún turned to look at him.

"Whatever are you doing here?" he coughed.

Gammel wiped tears from his eyes. "Anda. She called to me." He smiled. "It appears we have much to discuss." The elf shook his head. "That girl will either be your downfall or your salvation. Either way, your heart beats solely in her hands."

Dagsbrún managed a small smile and rubbed his head. "Indeed. Where is she?"

Gammel's smile disappeared. "Behind you."

Dagsbrún turned and saw Anda lying by his side. He pushed himself up and reached for her body.

Scooping her up, he held her to his chest. "Gammel, what happened?" he turned to the elf. "

Gammel stood to his feet. "Nothing more than exhaustion. She brought back Gréasáin. How did she do it?"

Dagsbrún gathered Anda in his arms and stood. "Dhia. And Waymaker." He looked at Gammel pensively. "Are you sure she will be all right?"

Gammel pulled a small bottle from his cloak and removed the cap. "Anda met Dhia." His eyebrows raised in surprise. "Well, well. There is more to her than we ever gave her credit for. And Waymaker? We all thought that weapon had been lost." He turned the bottle upside down and dipped a dab of the contents across Anda's forehead.

"She has been a wonder, Gammel," Dagsbrún sniffed. "She waded into the tar pits to recover the sword. She ran it through the Cleite tree without hesitation. She, the weakest of us all when it comes to strength."

"But the strongest when it comes to heart," Gammel chuckled. He touched Anda's cheek. "Come on, halfling. Up you get."

Anda sighed and moved about in Dagsbrún's arms. Her eyes fluttered and then opened, and she looked up at him and smiled. "I remember being on the ground." Her eyes grew wider, and she gripped his neck. "And you... you were wounded! The arrow!"

"I was more than wounded. I am certain I was dead."

She wriggled in his arms. "But how..."

Dagsbrún set her down gently. "Someone summoned help." He nodded toward Gammel.

Anda remembered laying nearly unconscious and wishing that Gammel would come. She took his gnarled hand in hers and kissed it gently. "I did not think you would. Nor that you even could."

Gammel kissed her head tenderly. "Always for you, Anda. Always."

Dagsbrún gently wrapped his arm around her waist. "Come," he said. "You have a new age to usher in."

Anda looked down at Rioghail and Wampyr, lying still in death. "May the world never become this evil again."

Gammel sighed. "It will, my child. It will."

They walked slowly toward the castle. "Then this all will have been for nothing," she replied.

Gammel shook his head. "Nonsense. This is a story that mattered. That *will* matter. When elves and vampires alike sit with their children and recount the Vale's times long past, they will tell this story. Your story, Anda. They will tell of your journey, how you retrieved the Waymaker, and how you brought peace by restoring Gréasáin."

Anda sighed and gazed over her shoulder at the sword, embedded until the next legend would come and retrieve it to save the world again. "Truly, I do not know what I even did."

Dagsbrún. "Anda, you are far too modest. You have fled your home, survived my intolerable behavior, learned how to control your magic, crossed time, and space to enter another world, survived that world, and restored it to peace."

"But that is just it," she replied. I did those things simply because I had to. There was nothing magnificent about any of it."

Gammel looked back at her. "And that is your greatest attribute, Anda. For it is often the meekest of creatures that perform the greatest feats. Gréasáin could not have been restored by a royal elf, or rogue vampire. It had to be someone who believed they had nothing to gain from bringing back peace, someone with only the purest intentions. Gréasáin would have recognized no one else as worthy enough. Your willingness to give up everything for a world that was not yours was the sacrifice needed."

Anda was silent. "Now that it is over, it feels as though nothing has happened. And yet, in my mind, I know that is not true."

Dagsbrún took her hand. "You think nothing has happened? You have captivated a heart that does not even beat." He stopped and turned, gripping her shoulders. "You whispered me back into an existence worth living. You saw something in me I could not see for myself. You risked your life over and over to save this world. My world. I am immortal; my life spans out before me for infinity. And I dreaded each moment. But now, I would rather breathe an infinite number of breaths if you and I breathe together."

Anda had listened to words, enraptured by every syllable. Now she lifted her eyes to his face, tears brimming in her eyes. "I only meant I had done nothing of consequence. And I stand by that. For one, life given for the sake of many is what our nature should be, and therefore, we should only be remembered not for doing something heroic but simply for *doing* it." She tenderly kissed his hand. "If I am remembered for anything, then let it be that I loved you. And that your charm—animalistic, roguish, brusque... passionate, and full of love—made me love you even more. We do not choose for whom our hearts beat, but our souls choose for us." She touched her chest. "And my soul and heart are yours."

Dagsbrún took her in his arms as the sun broke through the shadows and kissed her. He did not care that Gammel stood by their side, watching as though he knew this moment would come. Nor did he care for the eyes watching from the castle walls. All he cared for was that she was in his arms, her lips pressed against his, their lives entwined like the rooted branches of an ancient tree.

Chapter 24

When they arrived at Castle Scath, the halls were in an uproar. Elves were fighting Vampires with both fists and weapons. No one noticed the trio enter through the main door and cross to the main hall.

"What are we going to do?" Anda asked. "They do not realize the Gréasáin has been restored."

"We must tell them," Gammel pushed through the throng.

"But will they listen?" Dagsbrún pushed an elf out of the way.

They heard a shrill whinny and turned to see Vandre astride Droime, running towards them. Droime trampled both elf and vampire underfoot, trying to get to Anda.

Get on my back. Droime reared up on his hind legs in front of Anda.

Anda grabbed the kelpie's mane and jumped up behind Vandre. She looked down at Gammel and Dagsbrún. "Follow me!" she yelled.

Droime plunged through the throng toward the dais at the end of the hall. He leaped up the steps and stopped in front of an immense throne carved from wood and etched with a series of expressive faces. He reared up once more, and Anda slid off his back.

Anda climbed up on the throne and stood with her feet planted on the arms. She surmised the crowd and shouted with all the strength left in her. "Stop!"

Silence rippled across the room in a heaving wave. All eyes turned toward Anda, more so out of surprise than a willingness to obey. Dagsbrún and Gammel pushed to the front of the crowd and stood at the base of the dais.

"What do I say?" Anda whispered.

Gammel turned around and smiled. "Your heart, Anda. Tell them your heart."

Anda swallowed. She was past the point of exhaustion. Her head pounded, and her body was drained of strength. She was not an orator; she could not even call herself a soldier. What could she say to the audience now waiting for her to speak? She breathed deeply, squared her shoulders, and dared to open her mouth.

"I am…" Her voice cracked, and the crowd tittered with laughter. "I am nothing. You would call me halfling. The village where I lived called me a witch. I see nothing within me that would warrant being chosen, much less seen as anything other than insignificant." She cleared her throat. "But in these last few weeks, I have learned that the measure of a person is not how they can conquer and reign, but how they can love and serve. The condition of our hearts is not what we take, but what we give." And in my humbleness, the Gréasáin saw fit to choose me. In my chaos, Gammel the elf saw how to center and teach me." She turned to Dagsbrún. "In my weakness, Dagsbrún, son of Raefn, saw the chasms of my heart."

"What do we care for you or your heart?"

The crowd murmured and looked about for the source of the voice. Elf and vampire alike parted as Bearla approached the dais. Gammel held his staff out, and Dagsbrún placed himself between Anda and Bearla. Bearla pushed Gammel aside and climbed the stairs, pushing against Dagsbrún to get to Anda.

"Go back to your people, Bearla," Dagsbrún pushed her back.

Bearla slapped him hard across the face. "My people?" she shoved a finger in his face. "Our people. You are half-elf, lest you have forgotten." She turned back to Anda. "What gives you the right to come here and govern us? You, who has never fought and lost those you love to this war?"

Anda stepped down from the throne. "I do not claim any right to Dorchadas or Calina."

Bearla's face twisted in pain. "You came here, spreading your naivete and goodwill." She turned and looked at Dagsbrún. "Seducing, manipulating!"

"That's enough, Bearla!" Dagsbrún gripped her shoulder.

"You killed my brother!" she screamed, pounding his chest. "Rioghail is dead because of you!" She sank to the floor, sobbing.

Anda stepped down from the dais. "Rioghail is dead, it is true. But so is Wampyr. And I believe their death should be an example. Elf killing vampire, vampire murdering elf... There is nothing good that comes of it. I have crossed from one world to the next, I have retrieved Waymaker, and I have plunged it into the heart of the Cleite Tree. I have done all the Gréasáin called me to do." She knelt beside Bearla and gently took her hand. "I am not a diplomat, nor am I queen." Bearla looked up at her. "But you are."

Bearla sniffed. "Whatever do you mean?"

Anda stood and looked back over the crowd. "If the Gréasáin has given me any power at all, I use it now to make this proclamation. Bearla is the rightful heir to the throne of Calina. She will the elven lands in her brother's stead. All will recognize her authority," She looked down at Bearla. "And her wisdom."

Bearla lowered her eyes and bit her lip. "I do not know what to say," she whispered. "I cannot accept this."

Anda offered the elf her hand. "It is your right. It is who you were born to be." She turned to the crowd. "Does anyone challenge this?"

There was no response but silence.

She turned back to Bearla. "It seems you have no choice." Anda pulled Bearla to her feet. "Rise, Queen of Calina." She embraced the elf and whispered in her ear. "Shall we be friends now?"

Bearla pulled away and looked into Anda's eyes. "It would be far easier than being enemies."

Dagsbrún bowed to Bearla. "My lady queen."

Bearla smiled wryly. "It does not sound quite so magnanimous coming from you." She took his hand and touched it to her forehead.

"Bearla," Dagsbrún muttered. "Your title will get you nowhere with me. I belong to another."

She laughed and turned to Anda. "And what of Dorchadas?"

Anda had not thought that far. Naming Bearla had simply been a gamble to appease a grieving sister. She knew who the obvious choice was, but she was terrified to say it out loud. She looked to Gammel for guidance. He looked back at her knowingly, leaning on his staff, his eyes shining with merriment.

Anda reached out and took Dagsbrún's hand. "Dorchadas belongs to the vampire, as it has for a millennium. But the Vale is not just elf or simply vampire. It is both. And so, what better testament to the peace and unification that has been restored than to have both reign in Dorchadas." She raised Dagsbrún's head above their heads. "Let Dagsbrún, son of Raefn, rule in his godfather's stead. Let his name restore peace between the vampire and elf, as his parents wished to do so many years ago with their union."

Dagsbrún pulled his hand down. "Anda, I cannot accept."

She smiled. "Why ever not?"

He looked out at the crowd and then back at her. "Because I am a pariah in this world." He hung his head. "I am a pariah in your world. Everywhere, I am shunned whether it is for my lust for blood, or that I am my parent's son."

Gammel whirled around. "Oh, poppycock!" Anda and Dagsbrún looked at him, taken aback by his choice of words. He shifted his weight against his staff and sighed. "Dagsbrún, I was there. I was there when your parents died in one another's arms." He turned to the crowd. "And for what? Laws so old none of us, even those who are ancient, can remember? Rules that shut one species off from the other because one lives in the light, and the other, in darkness. I have raised this boy since he was an infant and watched him struggle against the appetite of his father and the gentility of his mother. There is no vampire nor elf that has been more conflicted about the face he wears, than Dagsbrún. He wrestles with himself day to day because he does not want to deny his mother or his father the honor of being as much like them as he can." He paused. "But the truth is, he is not Raefn, nor even Ljosalfar. He is the perfect mixture of both. For is night a child of the darkness, nor a child of the light."

Anda looked at Dagsbrún—his heart, strength, and love for her. She leaned her head on his shoulder and whispered, "He is a child of the dawn." She turned her face to the crowd. "Dagsbrún has protected me with his life. Indeed, he died for the sake of the Gréasáin, only to be restored by it. If that does not merit him to at least have a chance to lead the vampire, then surely there is none worthy to reign in Dorchadas."

The hall echoed with the last syllables of her words Anda feared she had said too much. She buried her head in Dagsbrún's shoulder, wishing she could disappear.

And then, a murmur went through the crowd, soft and low. "Dagsbrún, Dagsbrún, Dagsbrún."

Anda turned her head to listen. The murmur turned to a low rumble. Dagsbrún, Dagsbrún."

She turned and looked at the crowd, reaching out and touching Gammel's shoulder. She could see that his eyes were filling with tears. She turned back and looked at Dagsbrún. "Well, what say you Dagsbrún, Child of Dawn?"

He looked at her, full of wonder. His mouth half curved into a smile. He shook his head and threw up his hands. "What can I say to counter you, Anda? You have been, and always will be, right." He turned to the multitude and shouted, "I accept!"

The hall erupted in cheers and applause. Their words had once again realigned. Their reverie echoed all the centuries of strife and fear... gone with the act of someone with only one foot in their world.

Dagsbrún enveloped Anda in his arms, laughter coursing through his body. "I love you," he whispered.

She looked up at him, eyes filled with curiosity. "Why are you laughing?"

He gripped his face in his hands. "Because when I look at you, I smile. And when I smile, I feel like there are a thousand secrets we share between us. We have found the thing the whole world has been searching for." He pulled her against him. "You are the tiny spark that made wildfires, and I adore you for it."

Anda touched her forehead to his chin. "Truly, you feel so familiar. As though I have loved you a thousand lifetimes."

Dagsbrún kissed the top of her head. "Let us start with one lifetime, and then consider the rest."

Vandre walked up beside them and cleared his throat. "Seeing as how you have created a haven for elves and vampires, perhaps you would want to take a respite? Together?"

Anda laughed. "But where would we go?"

Gammel sat down on the steps. He was weary, as though his life had been spent, but his heart continued to beat. His head was empty of all thought, and his bones were heavy and worn. He looked up at Dagsbrún and Anda, filled with relief and pride.

In his long life, he had never thought his grandson would find peace. And now, the woman who had given it to him had given it to all the Vale. He reached up and touched Anda's arm.

"Go back where it all began. Go back to Castle Skog."

Anda looked at Dagsbrún. "But your place is here."

Vandre brought Droime to them. "Let them celebrate for a few days. You deserve a moment to breathe. Droime will take you."

Anda embraced Vandre. "You have been the kindest of friends, Vandre."

He pushed her away. "This is not goodbye. I fully intend to follow you to Castle Skog." He smirked. "It should be quite lovely without the Vondod."

"But the portal?" Anda looked at Gammel. "How do we cross over?"

He stood. "Give an old elf some credit. My bones may be old, but my magic is not."

Anda threw her arms around him and kissed him on his weathered cheek. "Thank you. For everything."

He tenderly stroked her head. "It was you, Anda. You did it all."

She shook her head. "No, you began long before I was even born." She looked at Dagsbrún. "You saved him."

Droime gently nuzzled her shoulder. *Shall we go?*

Anda smiled and reached up to pet his nose. "All right, Droime, all right." She turned back to Gammel. "Will you come?"

He shook his head. "I will stay and help reinstate the order. But never fear, when you reach the portal, it will be open for you."

Anda climbed onto Droime's back. "But how will you know?

Gammel let out a long rumbling laugh. "I always know." He lay his hand on Droime's neck. "You are all this world could have hoped for, Anda. This world, and yours."

She smiled with tears in her eyes and turned Droime toward the door. The kelpie leaped down the steps and walked towards the door, Dagsbrún and Vandre alongside her. The revelers parted for them, and a cheer went up among them. As they reached the door, Anda turned her head one last time to look back at Gammel, at Bearla, and all she had done. For the first time in her life, she felt a sense of contentment with herself.

An elf led two horses to the door for Dagsbrún and Vandre. They mounted them and the party turned once more to the East and the long journey back to Castle Skog. The cheers echoed through and out of Castle Scath in their ears as they crossed the plains of Dorchadas.

As they reached the border between Dorchadas and Calina, they stopped to watch the sunset. The hues of the sky were golden and amethyst, blended in twilight's embrace. A breeze whispered dreams across the grasses, and all of nature held its breath in wonderment of the heavenly masterpiece.

Dagsbrún brought his horse alongside Anda and reached out to touch her cheek. She turned and looked at him, her eyes reflecting the brilliance of the sky.

"Do not move," he breathed across the surface of her skin.

"Why?"

"Because I love you," he replied. "Because you chose me, and I chose you. And for a hundred lifetimes, in a hundred worlds, I would still choose you. Through any nightmare or chaos, I would find you and choose you. And knowing that—knowing I have found my answer—is the greatest joy I could possibly possess."

She smiled wryly. "I thought I did not belong to you."

His lips traced her cheekbone toward her lips. "You do not. I am yours. Completely."

Anda leaned in and let her lips graze against his. "Then try to keep up."

Droime reared up on his hind legs and dashed away across the meadows. Dagsbrún chuckled and raced after her, followed by Vandre, who knew his life would never grow dull following such a pair. They leaned into the warm breeze. The sun was at their back, setting them alight with glory. This world was theirs to revel in. This time was theirs to possess.

That, and a thousand lifetimes like it.

Made in the USA
Columbia, SC
14 October 2024